Twanna Underground

by
Cynthia J. Olson

PublishAmerica
Baltimore

First printing

ISBN: 1-4137-0642-8
PUBLISHED BY PUBLISHAMERICA, LLLP
www.publishamerica.com
Baltimore

Printed in the United States of America

Dedication

To all my students, Past – Present – Future.
To Ramona and her classmates.
And in memory of Malcolm.

Acknowledgments

I would like to thank all the people involved with this book. Gloria Rogers for years of support, Robin Bauer for the use of her computer the summer of 1993, Don and Lois Wilson, Eleanor Paul, Dr. Diane Kleckler, Ann Parsons, Anita Kososky, Kelly Stapelman, Brenda Muench, Adriane Dodson, Maria Marwedel, and Kate Niswonger for reading and giving feedback and encouragement. The entire Franklin family: Ben, Corenia, Nathan and Stephanie for giving me self-confidence when I had none. And of course, my own family: Richard, my husband and best friend, for always being there and giving me love, understanding and space to create, and Devin, my son, for making my life complete.

CHAPTER ONE

Twanna opened her eyes. Blackness greeted her. She could hear them fighting again. She closed her eyes and tried to make the sounds disappear. Humming softly helped. If she could just get her fingers into her ears, maybe she could go back to sleep. Her arms were stiff and she had to wiggle around to get her hands up to her head. She opened her eyes again. She wanted to make sure she was still under the couch. The musty smell of the old sofa filled her nostrils and blackness surrounded her. Slowly, silently, she turned her head.

Yes, there was a faint light.

It must be morning, she thought.

Was it time to get up for school? What day was it?

Oh yes, Twanna thought, *today's Thursday. School. Warm food. I hope we have turkey and gravy for lunch.*

Twanna inched as quietly as possible from her hiding place.

The voices were coming from down the hall. She knew her mother and stepfather were fighting again. She closed her eyes. Squeezing them really tight she could see her daddy. His big smile, his huge hands and she could almost feel the breeze as he lifted her up into the air, way above his head.

THUNK! Her neck snapped as her brother kicked her in the head.

"Get up, stupid," he snarled. "Get outa here."

Twanna scooted the rest of the way out from under the couch and tried to stand up.

The room was spinning and her head pounded. The red that came with the hurt was slowly fading and she could see her brother, Edward, slouched on the couch with a can of beer in his hand and a joint in his mouth.

Fear crept into her heart and set up housekeeping.

Twanna did not say anything. She walked backwards toward the kitchen, her eyes never leaving Ed's face. When she reached the kitchen door, she turned and ran into the room. She opened the refrigerator door and held it very carefully so it wouldn't fall off it's hinges. No milk. She slammed the door and pressed against it so it would stay. She turned to the cabinet and pulled the chair over to stand on. She climbed up and opened the door. No cereal. No bread. No breakfast. Nothing to eat. Nothing new.

She smoothed her blouse and tried to get the dust off her slacks. She wished again for jeans. She had a sweater but it was in the bedroom and she didn't want to go down the hall and into the dark noisy bedroom. She could wear these clothes again. She ran water onto her hands and wiped them over her face. No towel. Oh, well.

Carefully unbuttoning her blouse, she turned it around. She carefully buttoned it up the back. There, that was better. Maybe no one would notice it was the same blouse.

Standing in the kitchen doorway, she eyed the front room. Edward was on the couch. Martin was on the floor by the front door, Torrell was in the old chair, snoring, beer drying on his shirt, the can still lying on his chest.

Very, very, quietly, Twanna tip-toed past them all, barely daring to breath. She even willed her heart to beat silently – but terror defied her command and her heart pounded so loudly she was sure everyone would hear it.

As she got to the door of the apartment, she snatched her jacket off the hook, dashed out the door and fled down the stairs, hearing the slam of the door behind her. She slammed out through the entrance door and ran down the street and around the corner. She raced into the church yard and behind the brick wall of the bell tower. She hugged the wall and panted. She put on her jacket, pulling the hat from the sleeve, and slid down the wall onto the cement. Hugging her knees, she waited.

Dreams, ideas, hopes, flitted in and out of her mind. She tried to keep it blank. Seeing her cousin Martin had started that icky feeling in her stomach again. She couldn't stop the thoughts of the hurt he caused her. He put his hands on her body and hurt her. He put … she squeezed her eyes shut.

"No! No! No!" she silently screamed.

The earth trembled. Twanna's eyes flew open and her face lit up. The bells were ringing! She could hear them. She could feel them. She flung her arms around the brick tower and pressed her face against it. Her whole being was flying with the sounds of the bells.

The bells rang loudly and melodiously into the early morning air. The crispness of fall added to the sounds of the bells.

Twanna listened. She had to listen to begin counting at the right bell sound.

"One, two, three, four," she counted, "five, six, seven, eight," she waited. Silence. Just the echoing sounds of the bells.

"Eight o'clock. I'm early," she smiled.

Twanna stayed a little longer in the shadow of the steeple. The feeling the bell sounds gave her were still in her mind.

Nice feeling, she thought, *free, flying, wind, clouds, nice.*

As she started back out of the churchyard, past the old fountain where nothing but leaves gathered for prayer, she did not see the watching figure step quietly into the shadows.

The closer Twanna got to school, the happier she felt. Mrs. Edwards was her teacher and fifth grade was really fun. She could read very well and Mrs. Edwards had so many books.

"Oh no!" Twanna stopped. "Oh no!" she wailed aloud. "I forgot the book!" She began to cry. Would Mrs. Edwards be angry? Would she be punished? If she had to stay after school she would be very happy. But if Mrs. Edwards didn't let her take any more books she would just die! What could she do?

With a mixture of feelings, Twanna cautiously entered the playground. Maybe she shouldn't go in for breakfast. But her stomach said, "Oh yes you will, child!"

The hot breakfast program let her have a good breakfast every school day.

For free, she thought. Somehow that always surprised her. Her stomach was making loud noises as she stood in line trying to decide if she wanted orange juice or apple juice. She knew she couldn't have both, so she finally decided on apple juice. Next she could look at cereal, French toast sticks or pancakes. She mentally tasted each one. Which one should she choose?

"Hurry up, stupid," said an impatient voice behind her.

Mike, a boy from the sixth grade shoved into her. "Mike! If you bump into anyone again, you will have to get out of line," came the stern voice of Mr. Conley.

Twanna gave him a grateful glance, selected french toast sticks, a packet of maple syrup and chocolate milk. She turned to look for a spot to sit among the other students who had come for breakfast. The place was crammed.

Jaylin stood up and yelled, "Twanna! Over here!"

Twanna smiled and made her way between the long tables to where Jaylin was saving her a place.

"Hi!" said Jaylin, taking a spoonful of cereal.

"Hi!" Twanna answered, as she sat down and arranged her food on the table. Twanna moved her silverware around several times before taking a sip of her apple juice. She slowly dribbled syrup onto the French toast sticks, watching the sticky sweet liquid make miniature rivers on the plate. Then she cut off a piece of the French toast and popped it into her mouth. Her taste buds said, "Oh, yes!" She held the piece in her mouth and closed her eyes.

"Boy, does this taste good!" she said.

"Come on, hurry up," Jaylin was saying as she picked up her bowl of cereal to drink the milk. "I want to show you something."

"It'll just have to wait," said Twanna, sticking her nose into the air. "I'm dining!"

Jaylin snorted, then laughed.

"Twanna, you're a blast!" She got up to take her tray back and said, "When madam is finished will she please meet me at the swings?" She bowed to Twanna, who was also laughing, then sauntered to the front of the cafeteria to throw away her garbage.

"Sure," Twanna called after her, "but it'll be awhile."

"Very good, Twanna," Miss Hummel said, "I'm so glad to see you chew every bite carefully. I'm glad that you remember we discussed careful chewing helps digestion in Health class last week."

"Yes, Miss Hummel," Twanna mumbled. She didn't care

about digestion, she just wanted to taste each piece and enjoy it. She hadn't had anything to eat since lunch the day before.

Most of the students had already cleaned up and were outside by the time Twanna put her tray on the rack. She tossed her napkin in the garbage, with her paper cup and milk carton. She stopped on her way out to go into the restroom.

Twanna hated this restroom. Rows and rows of toilets. Each in a stall, each stall with no door. Some were not flushed and the smell was horrible. She held her breath and ran water over her sticky fingers. No matter how she tried not to, she got sticky fingers whenever she had syrup.

Letting out her breath and tossing a paper towel into the garbage, she pushed through the restroom door and almost collided with Angel, a girl from her class.

"Oh, I'm sorry," Twanna said. "I'm in a hurry to get out of there, it smells."

"Oh, and I suppose it doesn't smell like your house?" Angel raised her eyebrows at Twanna, tilting her head back and flipping her long blond hair in the process. She wanted to raise just one eyebrow but although she practiced a lot, she just couldn't do it yet.

Twanna looked at Angel, then at Marie and Lisa, who were with her. They were trying not to giggle. *Trying* not to giggle.

Twanna turned and ran through the double doors to the outside. *Not clean air, but better then the restrooms,* she thought, looking through the crowd of kids for Jaylin. Spotting her with Marvin and Walter, Twanna headed in her direction.

"What do you have?" she panted.

"Oh, hi, Twanna." Jaylin acted as if she was seeing her for the first time that morning.

"Hi," said Walter and Marvin together.

Marvin tossed an old looking tennis ball to Walter.

"Did you do that arithmetic homework last night?" Walter asked Jaylin, as he caught the ball. Returning the toss to Marvin, he looked at Twanna.

"No!" Twanna gasped, hands flying to her face. "I forgot!" she wailed. Now she was sure Mrs. Edwards would be angry. What could she do?

Jaylin said, "Oh, Twanna, what's the matter with you? Don't you remember you gave it to me to keep for you?"

A tidal wave of relief surged through Twanna. Yes! She had finished it before leaving school and had given it to Jaylin to keep for her. Jaylin had a really nice notebook with pockets to keep stuff in. She gave Jaylin a big smile that said thank you.

CHAPTER TWO

The bell rang.

"Ya know, that doesn't sound like a bell," stated Marvin. "It's just a loud jagged sound that really gets your attention." He shoved the tennis ball into his jacket pocket and trotted after Walter to line up.

As Jaylin and Twanna joined the fifth grade line, Twanna whispered, "What did you want to show me?"

Jaylin turned around to say something but saw the monitor looking at her.

"No talking in line, or you'll get a pink slip!" A pink slip would mean no recess. Jaylin shook her head and turned toward the front of the single file line.

Quiet settled on the playground. Scuffling of feet, some titters, some giggles, a sneeze, then silence. Mr. Conley blew a whistle and the lines started to enter the building. The fourth and fifth grade lines entered through the same blank metal double doors, filed up to the second floor and then split, the fourth grade left and the fifth grade right. Two lines of each grade, about twenty-eight in each line. They split again, one fourth grade line to the room on the left, the other fourth grade line to the room on the right. The fifth grade lines followed the same procedure.

The stairs they climbed were old, made of marble, worn where thousands of feet had marched before. The banisters were of wrought iron, painted a shinny black.

When the children entered their classrooms, the lines broke up and the ones who wore coats, jackets, hats, went into the cloak room. This was a long closet about four feet wide with hooks and shelves on both sides. There was a door at each end leading back into the classroom. The entire cloak room was oak paneling, with storage cabinets way above the students heads.

The class room itself, was very large. At one point in it's many years, desks had been fastened to the floor, in long rows. They had long since been removed and replaced with desks and chairs that could be moved into different work areas or circles. Mrs. Edwards had them grouped into fours. Two desks facing two other desks, making a larger work area, and students facing each other. One wall of the classroom was covered with tall windows, and one wall had a blackboard, which could be moved around to get into cabinets behind it. The teachers desk usually centered in the middle of another wall, was shoved into the corner of the back of the room, and used mainly for "stuff." Mrs. Edwards didn't sit down often, and never behind her desk. Sometimes she sat in the rocker which was in the reading area.

Twanna loved this room. The sun always came in the windows in the morning. The reading area had a book case with lots of books, two beanbag chairs, rug squares that could be moved around and the rocker.

The rocker was the place Twanna always wanted to be. The best reader, the student with all work turned in, got to sit in the rocker for twenty-five minutes during free reading time. Twanna was usually there, Jaylin got there sometimes and Walter was a contender. Angel wanted to get there but was not always right in her answers and she would tell Mrs. Edwards that she, Angel, was right, Mrs. Edwards was wrong, and Mrs. Edwards should go back to school or something. Angel was not rewarded for that behavior.

Twanna loved to read. She liked to do her work, so she earned rocker time often. Angel would get so angry and whisper that Twanna cheated, or that Twanna was teacher's pet. She would sometimes pretend that she "let" Twanna win because she didn't want to sit in the spot where she might get a *disease.*

"Everyone sit down, please,"said Mrs. Edwards.

The school day had begun.

When Twanna next looked at the clock, above the teachers desk, she was very surprised to see it was almost 12:00.

Already! Twanna thought. Her tummy growled. "I guess so," she laughed, almost out loud! She put her hand up to her mouth and looked around. *Whew! No one noticed.* She got back to work just in case Mrs. Edwards looked in her direction.

"Oh, boys, girls, let's make a nice straight line for lunch." Mrs. Edwards began the noise which consisted of chairs being shoved under desks, books being shoved into desks and bodies moving to the door to be first in line for food.

"I'm passing out the lunch tickets, Mrs. Edwards, or did you forget?" Angel flounced her way toward the teachers desk.

"No, my dear, it seems you have made an error. Bill's name is on the blackboard for "passer" today. And that wasn't an appropriate way to remind a teacher of anything. No, just control yourself."

Angel was scowling and just about ready to turn a really pretty face into a gargoyle look-a-like, when Bill said, "Aw, she can do it, that's OK."

The smile Angel gave Bill could have lit up downtown Chicago. Bill blushed. Poor Bill. The entire class had ammunition for the rest of the year. Mrs. Edwards, however, did not let Angel pass out the tickets, and the look she got from Angel was not at all angelic.

Lunch tickets were passed out, by Bill.

The long line of students wound its way down the old marble stairwells, deep into the bowels of the old building. The walls were green – the basement was green, the restrooms were green. Twanna didn't like this green. *It doesn't look like the grass or the trees,* she thought. *It looks – pale – sick – just not bright.*

The smell of lunch drifted up the stairs along with the noise. Talking wasn't permitted, but most of the kids whispered, some rather loudly. The band teacher was always on duty, ready with her whistle at the first hint of "unruly conduct." Twanna wasn't sure what "unruly conduct" was but she didn't want that whistle blown at her, so she kept in line and was quiet.

The food was warm. Twanna was starving.

"Wow! My favorite!" she whispered to Jaylin as they got to a spot where they could see what was being served.

They knew the menu said Turkey and gravy on mashed potatoes, but they never believed anything until they both saw it. Mrs. Peters, a big, happy lady, in a white apron and white hat was heaping spoonfuls onto the trays. She winked at Twanna and Twanna gave her a big smile. Twanna's plate was always just a little fuller then some of the other girls. The boys always had a big gob of potatoes and a ladle of turkey and gravy "just spillin' down the sides" as Mrs. Peters would say.

"The Ghost really likes you," Jaylin whispered to Twanna. She didn't want Mrs. Peters to hear because she didn't want to hurt her feelings. They called her the "Ghost" because she was so white. Her hair, her skin, her clothes, even her nylons and shoes were white. The kids liked her, but they called her "The Ghost" anyway.

As they sat across from each other, Twanna said to Jaylin, "How old do you think she is?"

"Older than anyone alive." Jaylin was putting real butter on her bread.

"No, I mean how old? Does she have kids?" Twanna was shoveling her food in. Jaylin looked at her.

"Twanna! What, you've never eaten before?" she said. "Take your time, savor it."

Twanna laughed. "Yeah, but I'm really hungry. I haven't eaten since…" suddenly she stopped and looked at Jaylin, "…breakfast," she said and laughed.

But Jaylin was looking at her plate. She felt her stomach do a flip-flop and tears started to cloud her vision. She knew Twanna practically lived in the street. She knew that if she had a mother, instead of only a stepfather, she could do something about Twanna, but she couldn't. She was lucky, wasn't she, that her stepfather wanted to take care of her but couldn't afford to "bring in the rest of the needy world," as he said.

The lunch hour was over. It seemed to go so fast, while the rest of the day moved like thick syrup. A washroom break was allowed and then back to the classroom. Science wasn't as interesting as looking out the window. Twanna knew she would have to read the whole chapter over but somehow she could not get her eyes back to the page.

"Twanna … Twanna … Twanna!" Mrs. Edwards was

calling her name.

Oh, no! Twanna thought, *I don't know the answer ... I don't even know the question ... I'm dead!*

"Twanna, I want you to stay back for a few minutes while the others go to the gym. Now, don't worry. It's nothing to look like that about!" Mrs. Edwards patted Twanna on the shoulder.

"What's it about?" Jaylin mouthed in her direction.

Twanna shrugged her shoulders and tried to swallow the lump in her throat. But her tummy was jumping and lunch felt like a rock.

She stayed in her seat while the other students got in line. Angel could be heard whispering, "Now she's gonna get it! I'll bet she got caught stealing!" The class just looked at Angel and Walter had to hold Jaylin because Jaylin was "gonna settle that girl right now!"

They left the room and it was silent. Mrs. Edwards came over to Twanna's desk. She pulled Walter's chair over and sat down.

"Twanna, I know life isn't easy for you. I just want to tell you if you need anyone to talk to, or you need something, let me know. If I can't help you, I will find someone who can."

Folded arms, head on arms, tears not staying in eyes but dropping onto the desk, Twanna said nothing.

"Mrs. Peters has been concerned about you for a long time, and we were talking the other day. She has some grandchildren about your size, and she…er," Mrs. Edwards hesitated, "she brought some clothes which will fit you. None of the other kids know about this," she hurried to explain, "but they are nice. Won't you come into the cloak room with me and see them? Please?"

Twanna jerked her head up. "Clothes?" she said. "Wow!" She scrambled out of her seat, brushed at her face, then pulled her already dirty blouse up to wipe her eyes.

"Oh, no! Twanna, use a tissue, please," sighed Mrs. Edwards.

In the cloak room, Mrs. Edwards pulled out two bags of clothes. Dresses, slacks, sweaters and sweatshirts. Even a jacket – a nice warm winter one.

"Purple!" Twanna exclaimed. She loved bright colors.

"But these look new," she said, "are you sure they are for me?"

"They sure do look new! And yes, I'm sure they are for you." Mrs. Edwards was having as much fun looking at the new clothes as Twanna was. "Oh, what a pretty dress," she'd say, or, "What a nice color this is for you."

The light slowly died from Twanna's face. She couldn't take these home. Her mother would find out and take them away – or something. She just couldn't.

Mrs. Edwards saw the change come over Twanna.

"Thinking about home?" she asked quietly.

Twanna nodded.

"I've got an idea," Mrs. Edwards said, leaning close to Twanna. "We need to work this out but why don't we leave these here and you can change when you get to school. We have a shower you can use – and Home Ec has a washer and dryer. We'll work out something. Okay? Now, cheer up and go to gym." Mrs. Edwards briskly began to pick up the clothes. She walked over to her teachers closet and began hanging things up.

Twanna joined dodge ball just in time to get hit in the head by a ball kicked by Walter. Jaylin was the first one at her side – it actually knocked her down.

"I wasn't aiming at you!" Walter was hanging his head – wagging it from side to side. "I'm just no good. I'm just a fool.

I wasn't aimin' at you. I was aimin' at Angel. Honest! I wouldn't hit you, Twanna. Honest."

"I know, Walter. It's okay. I'll be okay. Just leave me alone."

"Next time aim at Twanna, maybe you'll hit Angel," Jaylin snapped at Walter.

"Don't, Jaylin, he feels bad enough." Twanna knew how it felt to do something stupid.

Miss Hummel was slapping an ice bag on Twanna's head.

Gee, Twanna thought, *if I didn't need one before, I need one now. That hurt! And it's on the other side.* Aloud she said, "Thank-you, Miss Hummel."

CHAPTER THREE

School was over at about the same time as gym. They all went back to their classroom and "tidied up" as Mrs. Edwards called it. "Shovin' stuff in desks" is what they called it.

Then came five minutes of quiet. And it was quiet. No one was allowed to get into line until the whole room was quiet for five "peaceful" moments. Mrs. Edwards believed it was wrong to turn them "loose on society" without five minutes of down time. And she meant it! So they learned that five minutes meant five minutes. Not three, not two and one half but five minutes. Mrs. Edwards didn't have to say much after the first week of school. Five days of not being dismissed until thirty minutes after the rest of the school taught the lesson well.

As the kids hopped, pushed, jumped, shoved, and skipped out the doors, Jaylin said, "I wonder if he'll be there?"

Twanna froze mid skip. "Who?" she said, her eyes wide, her face scared, she looked at Jaylin.

"Your dog, you nut, *your* dog!"

"Oh," Twanna sighed, almost hoping it wouldn't be there.

"It's not *my* dog," she said.

"Tell him that," said Jaylin, pointing.

There sat the saddest sight. It's body too small, it's ears too large, it's face too pointed and it's ribs too pronounced. But eager, alive, and waiting for Twanna. Hundreds of kids passed by and it did nothing but wait – well, jittery waiting. When it finally saw Twanna a shudder went through it's too thin body and it stood up and quivered, waiting for her to get close enough for it to jump into the air, and fall at her feet.

"Jaylin, I can't have a dog," Twanna almost cried.

"I don't think you have a choice. The dog has you." Jaylin, the practical, smiled. "It must be nice to have a living thing love you the way that dog does."

The dog was going bananas. He was jumping, yelping, doing somersaults in the air.

Twanna said, "Somethin' ain't right. This dog has been trained." She tried out the thought.

"Sit." He sat.

"Stay." He stayed.

"Here." He pranced over to her.

"What's it's name?" A little first grader had wandered over to see the dog.

"Don't touch him, Tommy!" Tommy's mother yanked him away by the arm.

"Ouch! That hurts! I just wanted to pet him, Mommy," he wailed.

"He stinks! He's as dirty as she is."

The cruel words hit Twanna full in the face. She looked at Jaylin.

"She's a b----, she's not nice. If I could call her a nasty name I would!" Tears stung in Jaylin's eyes, for the sake of her friend.

"Do I smell?" Twanna was horrified.

"Not too bad." Jaylin hung her head. "It's been a rough day at school – we all stink."

"But, Jaylin, I can't take a shower – it's not safe…" She froze. She almost said too much.

Jaylin didn't seem to notice. She was making plans. "Come on home with me and bring 'Not my dog' too. We'll go downstairs to the basement – there's an old laundry tub where people used to do their wash. We can bathe him and ourselves. It'll be fun."

Twanna knew better than to argue when Jaylin was "plannin' fun."

Jaylin turned toward her apartment complex, waving good-bye, "See ya later!" she called.

Twanna and the dog trotted past the churchyard, turned the next corner and stopped in front of the building where she lived.

"Well, you might as well wait here. I'll be back and we can go to Jaylin's." The dog sat down.

The silence in the front hall was weird. The door to her apartment was unlocked. Twanna cautiously pushed the door open. She looked down the hall toward the bedroom. No sounds. She walked to the kitchen. No one there. No one anywhere in the apartment.

How nice, she thought.

She raced into the bathroom, but was afraid to stay. Instead she turned around and ran to the bedroom. She had one drawer in the dresser that was suppose to be hers. She pulled it open and ripped out some underwear. She turned to the closet, located a shirt and some slacks. The slacks were her mothers and she knew that they wouldn't fit. She looked under the bed and found her slacks from the other day. As she picked them up, she heard a noise in the front room.

"Oh, no!" she whispered to herself, "I don't want to be

caught back here."

She waited.

Someone had gone into the kitchen. Twanna knew this would be her only chance to get down the long hall, hopefully without meeting anyone. The hall was narrow.

She slipped as silently as a shadow, out of the bedroom and down the hallway. Quickly, without noise, she inched toward the kitchen.

"Who's there!" called her mother, pausing with a plate in her hand.

"Hi, Mom, can I go to Jaylin's?" Twanna held the clothes behind her back.

"Child, why do you smell so bad?" Her mother turned without waiting for an answer.

"You take a shower, you hear? And, girl, I don't want no excuses! Get out of those clothes now." She put the plate into the sink and reached up to the cabinet above, opened the door, and took down a bottle, half full of gin.

"Sure," said Twanna, beginning to fade away, "right after I come back from Jaylin's."

Her mother had already downed half a glass of gin. "Sure, okay, go away," she mumbled.

Twanna escaped.

Down the stairs, through the front entrance and out onto the sidewalk. There sat the dog, waiting for her.

Jaylin was waiting in front of her apartment building. There was a group of older kids sitting on the porch and the front steps. Twanna slowed down and tried to not look in their direction.

"Hey, Twanna! Did you bring supper? That dog'll have to put on weight before we can eat him!" The group laughed.

Twanna wanted to answer with a comment she had heard from her brother, but was too afraid to say anything.

"Come on, quick," said Jaylin. She ran toward the back of the building.

Twanna and the dog followed.

The apartment building had once been a fine building. Yellow brick on the outside, the apartments had been large two and three bedroom apartments, all of them having dining rooms, kitchens, front rooms and even nice balconies, and back porches. There was an entrance foyer that had once had a desk where apartment dwellers registered their guests, and an elevator in a wrought iron cage, long since boarded up.

Jaylin headed under the back porch to a door which was chained; however, there was no padlock on the chain so it slipped off easily and the girls, and the dog, entered a dingy, dirty, bare basement. This too had once been opulent. There were storage areas for each of the original apartments –about twenty-eight. The apartments had been split up, so there were at least fifty now.

In the dim light, coming in through dirty, small, casement windows, they could see a huge object with pipes leading in all directions.

"That's the old furnace," Jaylin whispered.

"Why are you whispering? Aren't we suppose to be here?" asked Twanna, nervously looking around.

"Naw, it's okay," Jaylin said. She laughed. It sounded strange and out of place in this dim, dank, world of cement, and broken bricks.

Going back toward the furnace, the lighting got worse.

"I know it's back here," Jaylin said. "But it's been a long time since I've been down here. I used to hide from … well, I used to hide here. It's kinda nice, when you get used to it. Down

25

here. Hidden. Alone. I used to like it. There!" She pointed.

Two old cement wash tubs, each with two sides, stood side by side. They were so old the color was mud. The faucets were rusty.

"Jaylin!" Twanna was disappointed, "How do we get water?"

"Turn on the faucets ... duh!" Jaylin reached over the basin and turned one faucet on.

BANG! BANG! BOOM! THUD! CLUNK! BANG!

Noise came from all directions! Twanna and Jaylin threw themselves on the floor, diving under the tubs. The dog began barking frantically.

"AIR!" Jaylin said.

"What?" Twanna hissed.

"Air. In the pipes," Jaylin said. "My stepdad had the water turned off to fix a leak in the kitchen. The pipes bang because there's air in them. I don't know why but that's what he said." Jaylin was standing up, brushing the dirt from her jeans. Twanna crawled out on her hands and knees.

"It's a good thing my clothes were dirty before – cause they're terrible now," she said.

Jaylin had had a bag with her. She retrieved it from where it had fallen when the pipes began to bang. Opening it up she pulled out towels, washcloths and soap.

"Here, let's see if there's hot water." Both girls braced themselves as Jaylin turned the faucet again.

Bang! Thud! But not as loud. Then some gurgling sounds and out came brown, thick water.

"Ewww! Ick!" Both girls backed away from the glop.

"I think I'll stay dirty," Twanna said, making a face.

But the water began to run clear. It began to get warm, and then hot.

"Well, should we try cold?" Jaylin turned the cold on with a flourish. It didn't make any noise and wasn't as dirty as the hot water had been.

Taking one of the washcloths, they plugged up the drain of one of the tubs and began filling it with water. They talked about washing the dog first. Turning around, they realized the dog had vanished.

"Call him," Jaylin said.

"Call him what? How can I call him when he doesn't have a name?" Twanna waived her arms.

"Well, give him a name!" Jaylin, the practical, stated, hands on hips.

"How can I name him if he isn't here? He probably ran away, I mean, he's not mine."

"He didn't run away. He's just … investigating the premises." Jaylin was sure. "Call him," she ordered.

"HIM!" yelled Twanna.

"Okay, smarty. You know what I mean!"

"Puppy! Dog! Animal that follows me around! Here, boy!" Twanna headed toward the entrance, convinced the dog had left.

"Here boy," Jaylin called, heading deeper into the shadows of the basement.

"He's over here," she called to Twanna. "He's found something. Ewww! I don't think I want to look."

Twanna hurried over to where Jaylin's voice came from. "It's dark. It's too dark, I can't see anything."

"Oh," Jaylin said and turned around. She ran back to the bag of stuff, pulled out a flashlight, turned it on, when nothing happened she slapped it a good one and a faint yellowish light flickered on.

She came back to where Twanna and the dog were standing.

27

Flashing the faint light around, they could see an old door, angled at a slant to the wall.

"It looks like a cellar door," Jaylin said. "My Auntie's house in Mississippi has a cellar door. It goes under the house and she keeps things cold down there."

"But why a cellar under a basement?" Twanna wasn't sure about this.

"I don't know. Let's look!" Jaylin, the adventurer, said.

"No way!" Twanna, the timid, replied, moving in reverse.

"Aw, come on, help me open this up, at least. I'll go in, you can stay here."

Twanna, very unwillingly, helped Jaylin pull the heavy wooden cellar door open. It was very old but held together. Some of the wood was rotten so the fastener fell apart. It offered little resistance.

With the door open, cement steps leading down were revealed. At the bottom, barely visible in the flickering light, another door.

"Let's not go any farther," Twanna said. "Maybe some of those other kids use this place."

"No way. Look at the dust," Jaylin pointed.

The steps were loaded with dust. The only marks were the ones Jaylin was making with her foot.

"We'd be able to tell if anyone had been here recently."

"Are you sure?" Twanna was still hesitant.

The dog wasn't hesitant. He was down the steps and scratching at the lower door.

"Come on." Jaylin was close behind him.

Twanna followed slowly. Caution was a large part of her being.

The lower door was, or had been, pad locked. When Jaylin took the rusty old lock in her hands and yanked, it fell apart.

"Wow! This was meant to be!" Jaylin, the sage, said solemnly.

They opened the door. The smell almost knocked them over.

"Ewww! Yuck!" they said as they pinched their noses together.

But the smell didn't stop Jaylin. Holding her nose with one hand she waved Twanna in with the flashlight.

"Come on! Don't worry. It's okay."

They stepped into a room which seemed large – and empty. Well, it seemed empty. There was coal on the floor.

"An old coal bin." They both slapped their heads and began to laugh. They had been afraid of an old coal bin. Well, an old coal room.

But the dog wasn't finished looking. He had gone out of the range of the flashlight and was digging. They could hear him. "Come on, boy. Don't find anything else. My heart won't take it," Twanna called.

But the digging noises continued. Suddenly they stopped and the dog barked. It was a strange sound in this half underground room. Dull sounding.

Using the flickering flashlight, the girls followed the sound of the barking. The dog was over toward a corner of the room, way in the back. The room still had some coal and the girls got dirtier and dirtier as they scrambled over the coal to reach the dog.

The flashlight was getting weaker and weaker.

"I hope this doesn't go out." Jaylin sounded nervous.

"Why? All we have to do is head toward the lightest part of the dark."

Twanna was sure of the way out.

Flashing the dim, flickering light along the wall, they saw another door. The dog was standing almost at a point, facing it.

"Well, look at the bird dog," Jaylin laughed, "Or should I say door dog."

"Now, we are not going to open that!" Twanna stated.

"Oh, yes we are!" Jaylin was already busy working at the handle.

The door opened – slowly, creaking on very rusty hinges.

There were more steps.

"If I were Anne Frank, I'd feel I had found a real life saver," Jaylin stated as she started down. "What a place to hide!"

"No! I'm not going!"

"Okay, just stay there. I'll be right back."

"Oh, no, you're not going without me!"

Twanna made her way carefully down the stairs behind Jaylin.

They were well underground. No light, except the flashlight, was visible. It was really dark. Twanna thought maybe she had closed her eyes.

They started forward, through the door, away from the stairs, into the blackness.

"Oof!" Jaylin exclaimed. She had bumped into something solid.

"Oh, look at this!" She turned the weak light on a crate. Moving the light to the side revealed something covered with a sheet.

"Well, in for a penny, in for a pound, my Auntie says." Jaylin took a deep breath, of stale air, grabbed the edge of the sheet and yanked.

Dust. Dust. And more dust. Choking dust.

When the air had cleared somewhat, and they had quit coughing, they raised the flashlight and stared in awed silence.

Under the sheet was a beautiful old couch. It looked like red velvet and it had wood across the back, in the front, on the arms and it had little carved legs on which it stood.

"Oh!" was all they could say.

The flashlight went out.

Jaylin slapped it, banged it on the ground, but it stayed out. Not even a flicker.

"Well, that's it for this trip," she said.

"No, I really want to look around." Twanna was excited.

"Look around? Well, maybe you could feel around. We need to go get some light – another flashlight, or something bigger.

"A lamp?"

"Sure. Where will we plug it in?" Jaylin sarcasticly replied.

"Oh, yeah. Well, I want to come back, don't you?"

"Boy, do I!"

"We can't tell anyone!"

"Maybe we should take an oath, or something."

"Naw, I'm not going to tell anyone and I know you won't either."

Each girl knew they had no one to tell, but each other.

"Boy, this is really exciting!"

"We have to hide the door with the coal."

"Oh, I can't see."

"Ouch! That's my foot!"

"I'm sorry."

"Where's the dog?"

"Here boy."

"He's in the doorway."

"Okay, push more coal over here."

"Head toward the light."

"That sounds like a line from a movie."

CHAPTER FOUR

When they returned to the basement they were more than just dirty, they were covered in black coal dirt. But the air around them was not only filled with dust, it was filled with excitement.

"Jaylin?"

"What, Twanna?"

"Did that really just happen, or were we pretending."

"Well, this coal dirt is real. I need a bath too."

"The water!" Twanna threw both hands up to her face.

"There'll be a flood!" Jaylin headed toward the laundry tubs.

Water was spilling over the sides and running happily across the floor and down the drain. Jaylin turned the faucet off. The water continued to run over the side but soon stopped. Most of the extra water had gone into the connecting tub and down the drain.

"It could have been worse," Jaylin said.

"How?"

"Oh, I don't know, but it could've been."

Jaylin began struggling with the dog, trying to lift him into the tub of water. He resisted.

"Now, a name for this dog!" she panted.

"He's all black, with just a little white. I suppose Blackie is out."

"Blackie is boring. Look, even he doesn't like it."

"It's not the name, it's the bath he's not happy about."

"What about Snowball? The snow around here is usually black, at least in a day or two."

"That's a name for a cat."

"Well, he's a bird dog, what about Pointer?"

"No, that sounds … strange."

"Well, think of something then."

"What about Mr. Finch. A finch is a bird."

"That sounds kinda neat. Do you like it, Mr. Finch?" Jaylin looked into the dogs eyes as she soaped his dejected head.

They slopped water all over. They lifted Mr. Finch into the empty tub and rinsed him off. It seemed to be a signal. He jumped from the tub and sprayed both girls as he shook himself from head to long black tail.

"Oh, stop that, Mr. Finch," Twanna said. The dog stopped, went to Twanna and sat down.

"I guess that's his name." Jaylin didn't sound too excited, but after all, he wasn't her companion.

"Mr. Finch." Twanna tried it several times. Each time she said the name, the dog looked up at her and wagged his tail. "Okay, that's it. You are now known as Mr. Finch."

The water had been draining out of the tub. Twanna looked at Jaylin. Jaylin looked at Twanna. Yep. They both knew they would have to bathe down here or answer lots of questions.

"But I didn't bring any clothes to wear," Jaylin moaned.

"Maybe we can split these between us – so we both have

some clean and some dirty."

"Okay. It's just my jeans and sweatshirt that are dirty, my underwear didn't get coaled."

The tub was filled again. Jaylin found an old milk crate for Twanna to climb on to get into the tub. Twanna washed very quickly. She was afraid that someone would come in. Jaylin was next. Mr. Finch seemed surprised that the girls had gotten all wet too. He tried to help Twanna dry herself by licking the water off.

"Stop that, Mr. Finch. It tickles! Go away!"

Mr. Finch hopped back a few spaces and sat down.

"Don't let him lie down! He'll get all dirty again." Jaylin warned from the tub.

Twanna was dressing. She put on her clean underwear, Jaylin's dirty jeans and her own shirt. Jaylin would have Twanna's clean slacks and her own dirty sweatshirt.

"I know, you just want jeans," Jaylin teased. She put on the clothes Twanna gave her. "Give me the rest and I'll wash yours with mine. No one will notice."

"We have to make plans. I want to go back there." Twanna indicated the back of the basement with her head.

"Me too. But with light. What can we do? We need a real good flashlight. Maybe something like people take camping."

"Walter is a Cub Scout." Twanna was thinking aloud. "I wonder if he has one."

"We're not telling anyone!" Jaylin said, firmly. "No matter what!"

"Okay, I didn't mean we'd tell him. Just borrow it. If he'd let us. If he has one."

They gathered up the clothes, towels, washcloths, soap and headed toward the outside.

"Shove the clothes into this bag. We have to go around to the front to get to the apartment." Jaylin held the bag open while Twanna shoved the stuff in it. "Doesn't it have a back porch?" asked Twanna. She had never thought about a back way in or out of Jaylin's apartment.

"Nope. Just a fire escape. You can't get in that way, that's just for getting out."

"What about Mr. Finch?"

"Oh, he's allowed." Jaylin was out the door and headed toward the front of the building.

The front was empty. Both girls sighed in relief. The older kids made them uncomfortable. They weren't really mean, just not nice. And they always seemed to want to give the girls candy. But both Jaylin and Twanna knew it was drugs. Some kind of new stuff was being made at home and it just took one time to get hooked. Nope – not these two fifth graders. They were educated – in school and on the street.

They went through the foyer and past the old boarded up elevator to the stairs. Jaylin lived on the fourth floor, in the middle of the building. Her apartment had once been the dining room and bedroom of a larger apartment. The bedroom had been made smaller by putting in a shower and toilet. The dining room became kitchen, front room combination. The only special thing about the apartment was the balcony off the front room windows. It was real narrow, but the windows were actually doors and in the summer it helped cool the place off, at night. It was also fun to sit on the floor and watch what was happening on the street below.

As Jaylin unlocked the door, the smells of Indian cooking drifted down the hall.

"The new family is from India. They have a couple of little kids. I can't tell if they are boys or girls because their heads are shaved. I guess they do that in India, when the kids turn two."

Mr. Finch raised his nose and looked in the direction of the smell. He whined.

"I'll bet he's hungry," Jaylin said.

"Yeah. How am I gonna feed him when I don't even get sup..." Twanna stopped. She had almost said too much. Again!

"Twanna," Jaylin stopped, turned around and faced her friend. "I know," was all she said. She reached out her hand. Twanna put hers into Jaylin's. "It's okay. You're my friend."

"Hello!" Jaylin called. Both girls listened for a response but were greeted with silence.

"My stepdad isn't home. Come on in. Let's go raid the fridge."

Twanna felt uncomfortable looking into the refrigerator. It wasn't full, but it had more that hers did.

"What do you want?" came a muffled question. Jaylin's head and shoulders were in the refrigerator.

"What can you fix?" asked Twanna.

"Oh, I'm a real good cook. Who do you think fixes food around here? It sure isn't that ol' man I live with." Jaylin tossed her head.

"Well, surprise me. I'll eat almost anything."

Jaylin shut the refrigerator door and stood still for a moment.

"How about spaghetti? I'll fix a big batch and tell Roland it was for his supper. He'll like that."

Jaylin took charge, telling Twanna what to do and how to do it. Twanna followed directions. When Jaylin was browning the meat, Mr. Finch sat up on his haunches and begged.

"Twanna, look in that cupboard over there," directed Jaylin, "I think there might be a can of something we can give Mr. Finch." Twanna pulled a chair over, climbed up and looked into the cupboard.

"There's a can of soup, some flour, sugar, salt, tuna fish,

beans, corn, tomatoes, marshmallows – they look pretty old – peanut butter. Wow, you have a lot of stuff here. Here's some beef stew. The picture looks really good."

"What's going on here?" came a voice from the door.

"Oh, hi, Roland. I'm fixin' spaghetti for supper. Okay? And Twanna is going to stay. Can she spend the night? Please?"

"Supper – yes. Night – maybe. Who's dog is this? Jaylin, you know I don't want a dog." He knelt down to scratch Mr. Finch's ears, saying, "Hi, pooch, how are you? Helping the girls? Taking care of them? Good boy."

"Well, he sorta adopted Twanna."

Twanna, still on the chair, hadn't said a thing.

"What's the matter girl? Cat – or should I say Dog – got your tongue?" Roland, Jaylin's stepfather, laughed at his own joke.

"No, sir. Thank-you, sir." Twanna felt strange – caught going through this man's cupboards.

"Relax, honey, I don't bite. Let me know when supper is ready. I think I'll go watch the news." He turned and went back to the front room – which was only a few steps away.

"He's nice," whispered Twanna.

"I know. I'm lucky. If he didn't want me here I'd have to go live with my Auntie, in Mississippi, and she already has six kids of her own, and three from my other Auntie."

Twanna knew it wouldn't be fun living with all those cousins. After all, look what cousins can do to you and nobody will pay any attention.

Jaylin's voice broke in on her thoughts, "Are you gonna stay on that chair all night? Get that can of hash and give it to Mr. Finch. Tomorrow we'll figure out a way to get some money to buy dog food."

"Jaylin, I can't stay here forever." Twanna actually hoped Jaylin would argue.

"I know. But I've got an idea floating around in the back of my head. Maybe I can catch it later and we can look at it, Okay?"

Twanna opened the can of hash and put it into a bowl for Mr. Finch. He gobbled it down as fast as possible. His whole body lurched with each attack on the food. He finished, licked the bowl and looked at Twanna to see if there was more available.

"Boy, he was really hungry." Twanna suddenly felt a strong kinship with Mr. Finch.

Mr. Finch, realizing there was nothing more to eat, gave a little dog bow to Twanna and went into the other room to sit at the feet of Roland. The girls could hear Jaylin's stepfather talking to the dog and knew he was petting him.

"Doesn't want a dog, yeah, right. He'd love to have a dog," Jaylin was muttering. To Twanna she said, "Let's sit at the table while the pasta cooks. We can make some plans."

"Pasta?" Twanna looked at Jaylin.

"Yeah, that's the name for noodles. Didn't you know that?"

"No. I only get spaghetti in a can."

"Yeck, wait 'til you taste mine. It's really good. My mom taught me, before she…" Jaylin turned to the table and began getting it cleared off. "Seems as if everything gets dumped on the table."

"What do you want me to do?" asked Twanna, "Can I set the table or something?"

"No, not yet. Just sit down and let's talk about the place we found."

"Won't your … eh … da … won't Roland hear?"

"No, he goes to sleep with the 6:00 News every night. He sleeps until I call him for supper. It's like a nap or something. I guess old people do that."

"Okay. So what are we gonna do?"

"Well, I figured we could maybe go over to Walter's house after supper and see if he has a light. You know, a big one for camping. Then, if he will let us use it, we can come back and go down…"

"NO WAY!" Twanna cut her off.

"Shhh! Roland's not deaf! He'll hear you if you yell!"

"Okay, but we are NOT going back there at night!"

"Why not? It's dark in there anyway. What difference does it make?"

"Well … none that way. But I just don't want to go there at night. What if someone sleeps in the basement? They'd see us either coming or going. How would we explain?"

"You've got a point," said Jaylin. "But I don't think anyone has been down in the basement for a long time. Even the storage rooms are empty. Ya know, that would be a great place to stay if you didn't have a place to go. I wonder why no one has been there?"

"Maybe they have. Maybe they just clean up real well."

"Sure, Twanna, a homeless cleaning lady? Sounds a little strange to me."

"I just don't want to go there tonight." Twanna was emphatic.

"Tomorrow is Friday. Maybe Saturday we could spend the whole day down there. I''ll bet there are tons of boxes and stuff to go though. Maybe there are some real treasures. I mean, REAL treasures. Stuff we could sell." Jaylin looked at Twanna.

"Sell? But that stuff isn't ours. Jaylin, that stuff belongs to someone."

"I know, but what if we can't find any name, or anything to tell us whose it is? What then? Do you think we could keep it?"

"I don't know. We'll have to try really hard to find who it belongs to. Maybe we should tell the police?"

"What?! And have some adult take charge? No thank you. I don't want any adult to know about this. Promise me, Twanna, no adults. Even if we have to tell someone sometime, no adults. Come on, promise."

"I promise. It's not like I have an adult in my life to tell anyway. I mean, Roland would be the only one I know that I would even think of telling. Ya know, maybe a teacher at school would…"

"NO ADULTS!" Jaylin raised herself out of her chair and leaned over Twanna. "I don't trust any adults."

"Okay, don't have a hissie fit. I won't tell. It's your basement not mine."

"I wonder if any of the other big apartment buildings have anything like that. Maybe we could investigate some of the other buildings and find out." Jaylin loved a project … especially if it involved mystery. She read all the Nancy Drew books she could find.

"Well, let's find out about this one first. Maybe there isn't anything in there but old furniture. We sure couldn't sell that. But we could use it as a play room. Ya know, a room where we could go where no one would find us. A hide out. Nah, that sounds like a criminal. I mean a hide away. That doesn't sound right either … you know what I mean. A tree house underground."

"I know what you mean. And you could spend more time there than I can, because your mother doesn't…" she stopped, horrified at what she was about to say.

"I know. Maybe it would be nice to have a place to stay."

"Goin' somewhere?" Roland asked from behind them.

"No, we're just talking. You know, homework kinda talk."

"I don't see any paper and pencils. When I was a kid, we used paper and pencils. I suppose all that has changed. Do you have computers to use in school?"

"Yeah, we have one in the class room, and more in the library," Jaylin replied, relieved that the subject had been changed. How long had Roland been standing there? What had he heard? Jaylin really didn't trust any adult.

"I think the pasta is done." Roland had gone over to the stove and was swishing a fork through the spaghetti noodles.

"Well, go sit down and I'll mix the spaghetti and the sauce. Twanna, get the lettuce from the fridge and we can have a salad. Oh, I didn't make any garlic bread! I love garlic bread." Jaylin sounded really disappointed.

"I'll fix that, Jaylin, after all, I'm not helpless in the kitchen. You really do spoil me, always getting supper, cleaning stuff up, washing clothes. I really appreciate how hard you work little girl. And she gets good grades, too." Roland had turned and addressed the last remark to Twanna. "As if you didn't know. And that's another thing. I'm real glad that you two get along so well. It's nice to have a good friend. One you can get into trouble with and trust not to tell." Roland laughed. "If you could see the looks on your faces right now ... I know you must be planning something. I won't ask, but don't get into real trouble. I think you're both too smart for that. Remember, I'm here if you need me. Either one of you." Then he looked right at Twanna.

Supper was very good. Mr. Finch even got some leftovers. He seemed to like the garlic bread too.

CHAPTER FIVE

The night was crisp and very clear. Twanna and Jaylin walked close together through the crowded streets. The noise of the traffic, the sound of people talking, and the sounds coming through open windows of crowded apartment buildings, were sounds both girls were so familiar with that they didn't even notice it.

Suddenly Twanna stopped. She turned around and listened. The bells were ringing and she had to listen. Jaylin knew Twanna loved the sound of the bells, but she was in a hurry.

"Come on, Twanna, we don't have much time!" Roland had given them permission to go out for an hour and she knew she had to be back on time or she would be grounded. And she did not want to not be allowed to leave the apartment with the basement still unexplored.

Walter lived in a nicer neighborhood than the girls did. He lived in a house with a fenced yard. Inside the fence was a big old tree, in which Walter had built a kind of tree house. Just some boards laid across two huge branches and a ladder. But it was a place where they could talk and no one would overhear. Walter had four brothers and two sisters. Someone was always around. The girls knew where to find Walter.

"Hey, Walter!" Jaylin called up to the platform in the tree.

"Hi. Come on up," Walter called back.

When Twanna and Jaylin had climbed up the ladder and were seated on the floor, Jaylin asked, "What are you up to?"

Walter looked around, as if looking for spies and said, "I'm planning to run away."

Jaylin and Twanna were shocked. They couldn't believe that Walter would even think of running away. He had a home, a mother, a father, brothers and sisters, kids to play with, food to eat, clothes to wear. Why would he run away?

"Why?" they both asked at once.

"My Dad's leaving."

"Oh." Not much to say to that. Twanna and Jaylin were both quiet. They wanted to ask why, but didn't dare.

"It's my fault. If I weren't so stupid maybe he'd stay. But I can't do anything. I can't play baseball. I can't shoot baskets. I need my glasses all the time, and I always seem to loose them, or they get broken. I just don't do anything right."

"Walter, it's not your fault! People are always telling kids it's not their fault that parents get divorced."

"Divorced? Don't you say that!" Walter broke in. He was very upset. He kept rubbing his hands on his pants and then in his hair. His hair stood straight up and was really dirty.

Twanna and Jaylin looked at each other. There wasn't much for them to say.

"It'll be okay, Walter, just wait." Twanna wanted to help him so much.

"No. Nothing will be okay again. Ever." He sounded so depressed. They all just sat in silence.

Jaylin and Twanna had to run all the way home. Time had not been a friend and they were almost late. As they ran up the stairs to Jaylin's apartment they met Roland on his way out.

"I was just coming out to look for you two. It's not safe in this neighborhood for the two of you to be out after dark. I told you, Jaylin, one hour was all you had. You get yourself into that apartment. Come on, Twanna, I'm going to walk you and that mutt home."

"You don't have to do that. I can walk home by myself. I'm real close, sir. And I have Mr. Finch. He'll scare anyone off."

Twanna looked at the small little black dog next to her. He looked up into her face and wagged his tail. *Sure*, she thought, *You'll scare them off ... won't you, please*? She sent her silent plea through her eyes to the big brown eyes of the dog.

"Ha!" Roland gave a short laugh. "I'm walkin' you home, child, and that's that. Come on, say good night to Jaylin." He started down the stairs.

The girls looked at each other. Jaylin shrugged her shoulders to indicate she didn't know what to do but do what he said.

Twanna almost had to run to keep up with Jaylin's stepdad.

"I live just around the corner. You know, just past the church.'

"I know. It's too late for you to be out by yourself. What time did your folks want you home?"

"They didn't say," Twanna mumbled the answer.

"What was that? I didn't hear you?" He slowed down and leaned over in Twanna's direction.

"I don't have a time to be home," Twanna said more loudly. *I don't have a home*, she thought.

"Are your parents home now?"

"I don't know."

45

"Maybe I'll talk to them."

Oh,no! Twanna thought, *I'll die! What if Mom's drunk? Or what if they're in the bedroom again, fighting?*

She stopped. "This is it," she said.

The entire building was black. Not a light showed anywhere. There was a crowd of people in front of the building, all talking at once. Just about that time a squad car pulled up to the curb and asked what was going on.

One of the people in the crowd stepped forward, and Twanna could see that he was the neighbor across the hall.

"Fuse, Officer. Some dumb sonofa----- blew all the fuses."

"All of them in the entire building? How could anyone do that?" asked the officer, as he got out of his car and flashed around his flashlight.

"I don't know. But there aren't any replacements – this is the old type of fuse box, we don't have any fancy circuit breakers here. Nope, this cheap son-of-a-----owner wouldn't bring this place up to code. Nope, he'd really like to see this place burn to the ground. Insurance, ya know. He don't care about people. Alls he cares about is money. He sure is around for rent. Where is he now? I ask you. Where is that son-of-a ---- now? Not here, that's sure." The man was very angry.

"Calm down, mister," said the Officer. "Maybe this is a good thing. Maybe now the city will come out here and look at the old box and the old wiring and make the owner fix the place up."

Twanna suddenly realized someone was standing right behind her. She felt him rub his body against hers. She jumped and turned around. Martin was grinning at her.

"Come on in, Twanna. Oooh, baby, come on in. It's nice and dark and no one can see anything. Know what I mean?"

He smelled like stale beer and sweat. He tried to move up

closer to Twanna but was stopped by a very deep growl.

Mr. Finch was baring his teeth at Martin.

Martin tried to laugh, but something about the dog's stance made the sound die in his throat. It came out a sickly gurgle.

Jaylin's stepdad grabbed Martin by his collar and lifted him off the ground.

"What did you say?" he demanded.

"Nothin'! Mister, put me down! I didn't say nothin'!"

"Hey, what are you doing?" The Police Officer looked over in their direction.

"I am protecting a child from a skunk," Roland replied as he put Martin down. "Do you know him?" he asked Twanna.

"Yes, sir. He's my cousin." Her eyes told Roland how terrified of him she was.

"Are your folks here? Can you find your parents?" Roland was looking at the people in the crowd.

"I don't see them. I don't see my brother either." She was craning her neck to see, but she wasn't very tall. And it was very dark.

"Martin, Twanna is staying at Jaylin's home tonight. If her parents ask you tell them that, okay? Now, be sure you give them the message or I might not be as gentle next time." He turned away from the crowd, took Twanna's hand in his own and headed back down the street. Mr. Finch followed close behind.

Spending the night at Jaylin's was fun. Roland had to tell them to be quiet several times after the lights were out. They just could not stop giggling. And nothing was funny! They had to retreat under the covers to stifle the noises.

Jaylin and Twanna slept in the bedroom and Roland had the day bed in the front room. Jaylin usually slept there, but Roland said that girls need privacy.

"I've been thinking that we will have to make some changes around here anyway, before long. Jaylin will have to have someplace to sleep other than the front room. I don't know what we're going to do. Maybe I can put a partition in the bedroom and make two small rooms. I'll have to check with Joe, the janitor first, maybe he can talk to the owner."

"Jaylin," whispered Twanna, "Who's the owner?"

"I don't know," came the muffled answer.

"Maybe he would know who that stuff belonged to."

"No!" Jaylin sat straight up in bed, flipped around to face Twanna. "I don't want to ask ANY adult!"

"All right!" Twanna was surprised at Jaylin's reaction. "All right. Go to sleep. Don't worry. Good night. And, Jaylin?" Twanna was speaking softly, as she snuggled down with a pillow scrunched under her head. "Thanks."

"Okay. It's okay, Twanna."

Twanna seemed to be floating. Where was she? There was light all around. She could tell without opening her eyes. She slowly opened one eye and peeked.

"Oh, yeah! I'm at Jaylin's!" she remembered.

It was early. Jaylin was still asleep and she could hear soft snoring coming from the other room. She turned on her side and snuggled down into the bed, cozy under the soft blanket.

"I wish I could always wake up like this," she thought. "Maybe someday I will have a room, with a bed of my own. Maybe someday I…" She drifted off into a pleasant dream.

The next thing she knew, Jaylin was shaking her shoulder. "Wake up you sleepy head. Roland has to go to work and he wants us outta here before he leaves. We can eat at school. Come on!"

Twanna rubbed her eyes. "What time is it? What can I wear

to school? Oh!"

"What?"

"I just remembered! Mrs. Edwards gave me a whole pile of clothes, well, not Mrs. Edwards but Mrs. Peters," came the garbled response.

"Well, you need to wear something now. You can't go in my dirty jeans."

Jaylin was in the closet, throwing clothes in Twanna's direction. "Find something!"

"Maybe Mrs. Edwards will let me bring the clothes here." Twanna really wanted to share them with Jaylin.

"Sure, then if I showed up in school with something on that came from that pile, I'd have both Mrs. Edwards and Mrs. Peters mad at me."

"No, I'd tell them it was my idea."

"We'll see. Get dressed. You want to use the bathroom? I don't have a tooth brush for you, but there's a pick for your hair."

"I'll brush my teeth with my fingers. I usually do that anyway."

Twanna dressed quickly. She and Jaylin were ready to leave within minutes. Twanna knew how to move when necessary.

Mr. Finch had spent the night in the kitchen, and greeted them with wags and licks.

"What are we going to do about the dog?" Roland was standing by the sink with a cup of coffee in his hand.

"He can just stay outside the way he always did." Twanna didn't know what else to say.

"Well, if you take him outside right away, I guess he can stay in the apartment. It's not as if there was anything for him to destroy in here." He didn't seem to happy about something.

He leaned down and took Mr. Finch's head in both hands.

49

Looking the dog straight in the eyes he said, "Now, you be good! Don't you dare make a mess in here. Do you understand me?"

Mr. Finch wagged his tail.

As Jaylin and Twanna hurried toward school, Twanna realized she hadn't heard the bells. What time was it anyway?

"It's almost 8:20. We have to hurry if we want any food." Jaylin seemed to read her mind.

There was still plenty of food when they reached the cafeteria. And Walter was in line just ahead of them.

"What's n ... er, I mean, how are you today, Walter?" Jaylin blushed because she almost said the wrong thing.

"The same. I'm stupid. I can't do anything right. My sister fell outa the tree house and now everyone is mad at me. I wasn't even there! But it's my fault. And they're right. If I hadn't wanted a tree house she wouldn't have fallen."

"Is she okay?" asked Twanna.

"When did that happen?" asked Jaylin.

"She's okay. Last night, after I went to bed." He answered both questions in a monotone.

"What was she doing out there so late? Did anyone think to ask her that?" Jaylin demanded indignantly.

"It doesn't matter. I'm just stupid. I'd be better off dead."

"Walter! Don't say that! You have so much ... I wish I had as much as you do." Twanna was worried. Walter didn't sound right.

"What do I have that you want, Twanna? I'll give it to you."

A bed. Food. A mother who cares. Thoughts ran through Twanna's head, but not out her mouth. "Lots of stuff," was all she said aloud.

They had gotten their food and found three places together. Jaylin looked at Twanna.

"Maybe we should tell Walter," she whispered.

"What? You were the one who didn't want to tell anyone."

"Tell me what?" For the first time that morning, Walter looked interested.

"Well, it's a secret. We'll have to discuss it." Jaylin was almost sorry she had said anything.

"Don't tell me. I'm too stupid to keep a secret." Walter played with his food, eating almost nothing.

The whistle sounded and Mr. Conley told everyone to clean up their areas and get ready to line up.

Jaylin and Twanna gobbled the rest of their breakfast down as fast as their jaws could work. The three of them cleaned off their trays, dumped their garbage and headed toward the playground to line up.

School went as usual. Angel was nasty. Twanna earned the rocker for reading. Mrs. Edwards was in a good mood because it was Friday. They all got to watch a movie in the afternoon. It was the story about two dogs and a cat that found their way home through the mountains. Jaylin and Twanna loved the movie. Walter slept. Marvin liked the dog named Chance, and the girls knew he would try to talk like him for awhile. It would be funny.

During the movie, Twanna found a chance to speak to Mrs. Edwards about the clothes. She asked if she could take the clothes to Jaylin's home. Mrs. Edwards looked at Twanna for a moment, then agreed to the idea.

"But don't let Jaylin have all the good clothes, you make sure you keep some for yourself. It's wonderful to share, but it's a nice feeling to wear something brand new."

Mrs. Edwards also suggested that Twanna write a Thank-you note to Mrs. Peters for the clothes. It took Twanna a long time to write because she couldn't think of anything to say except Thank-you. And that looks strange on a large piece of paper. Maybe she could draw a picture of herself with new clothes on.

Mrs. Edwards glanced at the note and told Twanna to go to the cafeteria to give it to Mrs. Peters in person. Twanna was embarrassed, but went down the stairs to the basement. She found Mrs. Peters cleaning up huge pots and pans.

"Here." Twanna held out the card.

"Well, you didn't have to do that, honey." Mrs. Peters wiped her hands on her white apron, and reached for the note. Her face wasn't white, it was flushed and she had bright pink spots, not just on her cheeks, but all over her face.

Twanna just stood there. She didn't know what to do or say.

"Twanna, honey, I would like to do other things for you, too." Mrs. Peters continued, "I don't know what I can do, but if you need anything, I'd be honored if you asked me. If I could take you home with me, I would. Getting some good cookin' in your body, some flesh on your bones, and fixin' you up all pretty like would be lots of fun for me. But, I suppose your mamma wouldn't want anyone else doin' the things that are her responsibilities." Twanna really didn't understand what Mrs. Peters was saying. She just stood there, looking at the floor.

"Well, run on back to class, honey. Come see me sometime. I mean come over to my house for lunch, or supper. I live in the old house next to the church. You know, the church with the bells? I've seen you go there to listen. I go there too. They're wonderful aren't they? You'd think I'd get tired of them, sounding every hour and playing songs four times a day. And my living right next door. Almost under the bell tower, in the shadow of the steeple. But I love it, and I think you would too. So, come on over and spend some time with this ol' Ghost of a lady. Bring Jaylin if you want too. She's a nice girl too. A little wild maybe, but kind."

Twanna had a hard time taking all this in. Mrs. Peters called herself Ghost! She lived with the bells! She loved the bells! She wanted her to come over to eat! She knew Twanna went to the churchyard to listen to the bells. What else did this lady know?

Her mouth was open. Nothing would come out. "Ah, er, ah, okay," was all she managed to utter. Okay? What had she okayed?

"Thanks," she said. "I'll do that." She turned to leave and suddenly realized she really liked this woman. She felt the friendship being offered and suddenly really wanted it.

"How about Sunday? Can I come over on Sunday? After church? Please?"

"Land-a-Goshin', yes, chil'! That would be wonderful. I'll fix fried chicken for dinner. That okay with you? And mashed potatoes, gravy, and how about home made cranberry sauce? Pie, which kind, Apple or Lemon Meringue?" She seemed very pleased happy to be planning something that made Twanna salivate to just think about.

"Okay, Sunday after church. Thanks." Twanna waved her hand and headed back to her classroom. Mrs. Edwards looked up as Twanna entered the room, and smiled. Twanna glowed. Mrs. Edwards knew something special had happened.

Twanna looks wonderful, she thought, *It's nice to be treated as a special person.*

"Do you have to go home?" Jaylin demanded, as they left the playground after school. "What about Mr. Finch? He'll run away from me. Come home with me first. You can call your mom."

"No 'phone," Twanna stated. Deciding quickly, she said,

"Okay. I'll come over to your apartment and then we can take Mr. Finch with us to my apartment. And I can leave these clothes there."

"We? I don't like going over there. I don't like your brother or that cousin, what's-his-name."

"Please. That way I can leave again. My mom won't care if I'm with you," said Twanna. *She won't care anyway*, she thought.

"Do you want to stay overnight again. I'd like it, but I'm not sure how long Roland will go along with this." Jaylin was not going to upset Roland if she could avoid it. He wasn't the same person when he was angry. He never hit her, but it was scary when he was mad.

"Well, maybe. I was thinkin', Jaylin, maybe I could stay in the basement. It's warm and we could fix it up. I'd have my own home." Twanna was wistful.

"That's a great idea! In fact, maybe we could clean up that coal room and set up a play house. Well, not a play house, we're a little old for that, but a really neat place to go. We could get some lamps and some chairs…" Jaylin stopped – talking and walking. Standing in the middle of the sidewalk, Jaylin gave birth to the "greatest idea in the world!"

"That room! Underground! No one would find us! The furniture is already there! We could live there! Mr. Finch would warn us if anyone comes close!" Ideas kept pouring out of Jaylin's mouth.

Twanna just let her talk. They had been through "greatest ideas" before. However, this time Twanna wanted the plan to happen.

CHAPTER SIX

Jaylin refused to go into Twanna's building. "It's too scary," was all she'd say.

Twanna quickly went upstairs to her apartment. She was praying that no one would be there, so she could just leave a note and not have to worry about anyone saying no.

Loud voices could be heard from inside. *Oh, no!* Twanna thought, *more fighting!*

"Well, where the hell do you think she is?" came a loud masculine voice.

The answer was muffled, and slurred. Twanna knew it came from her mother, and that she must have been drinking again.

"I think anyone who has a kid needs to know where that kid is! Don't you even care, woman? That chile could be dead for all you know! Hell, throw that stuff out." Twanna heard a struggle. She was afraid to go in. She realized they were talking about her. Her stepfather was fighting with her mother about her!

"Hi! I'm home," she called as she burst through the door.

Oh, well, she thought, *Might as well get this over with.*

"WHERE HAVE YOU BEEN?!" Blasted her stepfather.

"At Jaylin's home and then to school." Twanna turned an innocent face up to look at his.

"And why didn't you tell us?" He sounded almost human.

"I did. I told Mom." Twanna turned to see where her mother was and saw her sprawled out on the couch with a cloth over her face. "Mom? Are you okay? Don't you remember? I asked yesterday after school?" She knew her mother had a hangover, but the scared feeling of seeing her sick still attacked her stomach.

"Huh, oh, well, I guess maybe she did ask. I think I told her she could go somewhere." Her mother remained under the cloth.

"I don't know, I just don't understand you." Twanna's stepfather shook his head. Twanna didn't know if he meant her or her mother.

"Can I go over to her home again tonight? And maybe spend the weekend? I'll do my homework, I promise."

"What about your chores? Who's going to clean up this – this dump." Her stepfather shrugged his shoulders. "I don't care. Do what ever you want to. I just give up."

Twanna had mixed feelings. She was glad she could go, but to see her stepfather give up was not a good feeling. Her mother didn't care about anything except gin, if her stepfather gave up and left, then there would really be nothing. How long before people are asked to leave if they don't pay their rent? Twanna was scared. She did the only thing that she knew how to do, said thank-you and left.

"Well?" Jaylin asked when Twanna came outside.

"It's okay." She really didn't want to explain the entire thing to Jaylin, right now, especially because she didn't quite understand it herself ... the mixed feelings of sadness, worry and happiness.

As they went toward Jaylin's apartment building, Twanna stopped in front of the church. She really wanted to go into the churchyard, where it was always so quiet and peaceful. The noise from the street never seemed to penetrate into the stillness of the church area – until the bells rang, however. Then the sound was awesome. It filled the entire world ... the immediate world of Twanna and anyone else listening in the churchyard.

"What are you doing?" asked Jaylin. "What are you waiting for?"

"Oh, nothing. Ya know, Mrs. Peters lives right there." Twanna pointed at the house next to the church.

"In that big old place?" Jaylin was surprised. "It must have thirty rooms. A whole bunch of people could live in there. Are you sure?"

"Yes, and I'm suppose to go over there for dinner on Sunday. Do you want to go with me?" She knew Mrs. Peters would have more than enough food fixed, she just knew it.

"I don't think I can. I'll probably have to fix lunch for Roland, and if it's a football Sunday, then I'll have to make sandwiches and stuff for his friends. Unless he goes over to someone else's house to watch the game."

A group of boys were standing on the corner. Jaylin and Twanna looked down at the sidewalk, hoping they would be allowed to pass without any hassle. No such luck.

"Come on, Twanna, show us your stuff. We're all here just waitin' fo' some fun!" Martin's voice cut into Twanna's soul, and terrified her. She did the worst possible thing. She stopped. She couldn't even move. She couldn't look up, but she couldn't walk away. Jaylin tugged on her sleeve. Martin kept saying horrible things, while his friends laughed and made noises.

Twanna was absolutely terrified.

Mr. Finch didn't even growl! He walked over to Martin and peed on his leg. Then jumped away as Martin tried to kick him. Martin was mad. The rest of the boys were still laughing, but now at Martin. Martin got madder. He came at Twanna to slap her. Mr. Finch jumped into the air and caught Martin's sleeve and pulled him away.

Jaylin screamed.

That sound released Twanna from her paralysis and she hit Jaylin on the shoulder as she cried, "Run!"

They ran. Mr. Finch ran with them. None of them stopped running until they were inside Jaylin's apartment. Panting, they all collapsed on the floor just inside the door.

"Running a race?" Roland was standing just inside the kitchen area, with a newspaper in one hand, and a cup of coffee in the other. "Or are the Hounds of Hell after you," he joked.

Both of the girls were out of breath and couldn't answer.

Finally Jaylin said, "Can Twanna spend the weekend?"

"Does she have permission?"

"Yes, sir, I do." Twanna was listening to her heart pound.

"Sure. I don't mind. You and Jaylin always clean things up and are usually very quiet. Just remember to go to bed early so we can get some sleep after the giggling stops. Jaylin, I'm going out tonight, so Mrs. Johnson will be here to sit for you."

"Roland. I do not need a sitter!" Jaylin was indignant.

"Jaylin. You do until I say you don't," Roland imitated her.

"But, I am eleven years old!"

"Not until January. And I won't let you stay alone until you're at least twenty-seven."

"I won't be alone. Twanna will be here."

"I rest my case!"

Jaylin knew when to stop arguing. And, anyway, she liked

Mrs. Johnson.

"Isn't Mrs. Johnson that old lady in the wheelchair?" asked Twanna, as soon as they were alone.

"Yes, and she's nice. She'll have treats for us and maybe she'll tell us some stories. She's good at that!"

"Oh, by the way," Roland called from the front room. "You are not to leave the apartment tonight."

"But what about Mr. Finch?" called Jaylin.

"Well, one walk, just outside where Mrs. Johnson can see you. Okay? You understand, I mean it," he stated firmly.

Together, Twanna and Jaylin both said, "Yes, sir."

CHAPTER SEVEN

Mrs. Johnson came into the apartment a little before 6:00 that evening. Twanna and Jaylin were eating sandwiches, as Roland helped Mrs. Johnson into the kitchen. The hallway was very narrow and it was difficult to get the wheelchair from the outside door to the kitchen.

"I hope you all like chocolate chip cookies 'cause I brung a big batch of 'em wiff me." Mrs. Johnson didn't like to wear her false teeth, and it made it difficult to understand her. "I done a passel o' bakin' today, it bein' nice and cool. I loves to bake in the winter." She grinned a toothless grin at them.

"Boy, is that what smells so good?" Jaylin asked. She jumped up from the table to help take the bag that was in Mrs. Johnson's lap.

Mr. Finch whined and sat up on his hind legs.

"Well, it's certain that one of you likes chocolate chip cookies," laughed Roland. "I've gotta go, see you later ... and all of you behave. You too Mrs. Johnson, not too many scary stories."

"My sakes, would you think I would tell stories? Just look at me. A poor cripple, with no teeth. Oh, I made some real good snickie-snacks, with pretzels and some of those round crackers, and cereal. I figure since it's made with breakfast food, we can eat it for breakfast, right. Heh, heh, heh." Her laugh sounded more like a cackle.

Twanna noticed Mrs. Johnsons nose almost touched her chin. Along with that cackle, she could play the witch in anyone's imagination. Twanna said nothing.

"Don' know what to make of me, heh, little girl?" She peered into Twanna's face. "Well, I won't bite ... that's fo' sure ... I ain't got any teeth. So don' worry." She grinned away.

"Are you going to tell us some stories tonight?" Jaylin asked hopefully.

"Maybe, maybe. But right now, I wan'ta sit and watch my program." She spun herself around in the wheelchair and moved quickly into the front room. She picked up the remote and turned on the TV.

"You like her?" Twanna was dubious. "Her mouth bothers me."

"Oh, she's fun. She just likes to act like that. She's okay."

The girls stayed at the kitchen table and made plans for the next day. Saturday. What a wonderful day. They could spend the whole day in the basement. The only problem was getting a nice big flashlight. Who would have one? Who would let them borrow one?

"Do you suppose Marvin might have a flashlight," Twanna was racking her brain.

"No. His mother never lets him go anywhere where he would need one," Jaylin said.

"Yes she does. He goes to summer camp every year. It's somewhere up in Wisconsin. I'll bet he uses a flashlight there."

"Oh, that's right! I forgot. He really hates it. He always writes letters that start with 'Don't bother to read this, I'll be home before it gets there.' I wonder why she still makes him go?"

"I don't see why he hates it. Good food, swimming, cool air in the summer. Sounds great to me."

"Me, too. I'd love to go to summer camp. I'd like to go to the ocean for summer camp."

"I'd just like to get away from here. I'd like to go to summer camp, fall camp, winter camp and spring camp. I'd really like to go to boarding school. You know, the ones we read about in the books at school." And with that statement Twanna's mouth hung open, her eyes widened and her hands flew up to her face. "Oh, No! I keep forgetting to take Mrs. Edwards' book back to school," she cried.

"That's what I had for you on Thursday morning! I keep forgetting too! I turned it in because you left it here. Remember? With your homework?"

"Oh, Jaylin! What would I do without you. Thank-you, thank-you. How can I repay you." Twanna was serious, but went into a dramatic stance.

"By giving me your life, peon, and," Jaylin turned serious, "By scrubbing the coal room floor."

"I thought we were both going to work on that."

"I've been thinking. Maybe we had better leave that room just as it is. If we clean up that room, someone might find it and notice, I mean, it would lead straight to the other room. We can't keep putting coal in front of the door all the time. We'd always be filthy."

"Good thinkin'! And less work." Twanna was glad Jaylin was smart.

"I don't know if we should take buckets down to the

basement tomorrow or wait until after we explore the room."

"I vote we wait. We might find stuff down there, then no one will see us and wonder what we're doing."

"So ... the main problem is getting a flashlight." Jaylin was pondering something, Twanna could tell by the softness of her voice.

"Girls!" came a loud creaky voice from the front room. "How about some snicky-snacks? I'm eatin' them all up."

Jaylin and Twanna headed to the front room and sprawled on the floor in front of the TV.

"Turn off the TV, Jaylin, and I'll tell you a ghost story," said Mrs. Johnson. "That is if you want to hear one."

"Sure, but we'd better walk Mr. Finch first. Okay? We'll walk him in front of the building so you can watch us from the window." Jaylin scrambled up from the floor, dusted crumbs off her pants and pulled Twanna up. "Come on, he is your dog."

Mrs. Johnson had made her way to the front windows and said she could see across the street to the vacant lot, and maybe it would be a good idea to walk Mr. Finch over there. The girls agreed but were a little afraid. That vacant lot was rarely vacant.

The trip down the stairs, across the street and into the vacant lot was uneventful. Nothing happened. The lot was really vacant. No gangs were around. The entire street was unusually quiet.

"Hurry up, Mr. Finch. This quiet is creepy," Jaylin said.

Twanna looked around. She couldn't see anyone. She looked up at the apartment building, and was strangely reassured by the sight of Mrs. Johnson's figure back-blighted in the window.

"What could she do, anyway?" Twanna asked. "She's in that wheelchair. I can't see her coming to our rescue."

"She can dial 911. And I've heard her shout at the older boys around here. She's not afraid to tell them to get away." Jaylin sounded proud.

"Well, if she had a gun under her lap blanket, then I could see why the boys listen, but they could push her down the stairs or anything."

"Twanna! Shut your mouth! I don't want to hear anything like that. Sure, it could happen, but don't say it, please!"

"Are her stories any good?" Twanna changed the subject.

"Sometimes. Sometimes she falls asleep in the middle and then can't remember what she was telling. It's funny." Jaylin was headed back across the street and hurrying toward the front door of the building, Twanna and Mr. Finch were right behind.

Suddenly, a group of boys came running around the corner of the building. They didn't even slow down, just kept running as fast as they could, past Jaylin, Twanna and Mr. Finch. Up the stairs and into the foyer, they ran. Jaylin and Twanna were surprised. So surprised that the sound of the car, as it screeched around the corner, didn't register in their minds at first.

Terror grabbed Twanna. She turned, grabbed Jaylin and threw herself down on the ground, pushing Jaylin in front of her.

Sounds of gunfire broke the once silent night into thousands of shards of noise. It was deafening. The car did not stop, but tore on down the street.

And silence again filled the night.

"Jaylin, Jaylin," screeched Mrs. Johnson from the fourth floor window.

"I'm okay," she yelled, from the ground, under Twanna.

Twanna sat up. She looked at Jaylin. Jaylin looked back from the ground. "Oh," was all she could say.

"Let's get inside! They might come back!" The thought put both girls into immediate action. They ran pell-mell into the building and up the stairs, two steps at a time. Mr. Finch was right next to them. By the time they heard the police sirens, they were already in the apartment, and Mrs. Johnson was hugging them.

"That's the closest I've been to a shooting." Jaylin was not only calmed down but was actually savoring the moment, after it was all over, of course.

The police had been to the apartment and questioned the girls. When the squad car had stopped, Mrs. Johnson had called to them from the window and they had come up. But neither Jaylin nor Twanna could tell them anything of help. They really hadn't seen who the boys were, and they hadn't looked at the car, they had thrown themselves on the ground. The policeman wasn't surprised. He hadn't expected to learn anything. Mrs. Johnson was able to tell him that the car had fins, which would make it an old car that had been restored. At the speed it was traveling it had to have had a new engine, a fast one.

Mrs. Johnson was making hot chocolate for the girls. They were going to have chocolate chip cookies, hot chocolate and then were going to bed. Mrs. Johnson said she would tell them a story another night. Too much excitement in one night was not good, according to her.

They were very quiet, both thinking their own thoughts as they drank their hot chocolate. The plans that they had been making for the next day seemed far away. Tomorrow ... at least tomorrow would come for both of them. This time.

CHAPTER EIGHT

The first sounds that Twanna heard the next morning, was a man singing. She kept her eyes shut and listened. She hadn't heard a man sing since her father had died. Oh, on the radio, sure, but not just an ordinary man. Roland sang old songs. Twanna didn't recognize them, but knew they were songs he enjoyed.

"He sure sounds happy this morning," Jaylin whispered to Twanna. "Sure different from last night."

When Roland came home last night, Mrs. Johnson had told him what had happened. The girls were in bed, pretending to be asleep, when he stepped into the room and looked at them. He was quiet until he got started talking to Mrs. Johnson. Both girls heard him complain about the neighborhood, and how he wished he had a better job so he could take Jaylin away from here.

Jaylin and Twanna had gripped hands at that. They didn't want Jaylin to move away. What would Twanna do? They scarcely breathed so they could hear what Roland was saying.

But, he complained, he couldn't move away. He would just have to watch Jaylin more closely and maybe talk to her about gangs and maybe even let her join a "kung-fu" class or something. What was the world coming too?

Mrs. Johnson agreed. She too wondered what was going to happen in the neighborhood, and in the city. "Not everyone can move to the suburbs," she said, softly.

The bright sun of the morning had brought with it new hope for a new day. Roland was not going to let the girls know that he was as concerned as he was. He didn't want to frighten them any more than they already had been. So, he sang. And he fixed French toast for breakfast. With bacon.

The aroma wove its way through the kitchen, into the bedroom and into the noses of two waiting girls. They both yelled, "BACON!" and jumped out of bed. They tore into the kitchen and Jaylin threw her arms around Roland, who was standing at the stove with an apron around his waist. Mr. Finch was sitting right next to him.

"Good morning, you two sleepy-heads," said Roland, breaking off in the middle of a song. "I thought this smell might get you up. Mr. Finch has become my best friend," he said indicating the dog, who was seated as close to him as possible. "He's just waiting for me to drop something, hopefully the entire plate of bacon!"

"Mr. Finch," said Twanna. "Come away from there. Be a good boy."

"That's okay, honey. I kinda like having him around. I heard about last night, from Mrs. Johnson. Do you have anything you want to talk about? Either one of you?" Roland kept his face away from them, busy with the bacon in the frying pan.

"No," Jaylin said as she got plates and silverware out. "We're okay." She handed the plates to Twanna.

Putting the plates on the table, Twanna said, "Nope. Me either."

"Well, we will have to have a talk about what's happening around here, but not right now. Let's enjoy breakfast."

Twanna started to sit down at the table but stopped and said, "I have to take Mr. Finch out for a walk."

"I already did that, Twanna. We went out very early this morning. It's a great day."

"Oh, I didn't mean for you to have to do that." Twanna was upset. She didn't want Roland to get angry or annoyed with her because of the dog.

"I enjoyed it. I need to get out and exercise more anyway."

They all sat down at the table and began to eat. Mr. Finch sat next to Twanna and waited, expectantly.

Roland was the first one to slip Mr. Finch some bacon. Jaylin saw him do it, but didn't say anything. She slipped him some French toast. Twanna was the only one who didn't slip him anything from the table … but she saved a piece of French toast for him, saying she was too full to finish it. Roland laughed and said he would be surprised if Mr. Finch wasn't too full also.

"What are your plans for today, girls," he asked, conversationally. "Fun?"

"Well, I'd like to listen to my radio, but I don't have any batteries." Jaylin kept her eyes on her plate. Roland was good at spotting a lie.

"Right. Well, there is a package or two under the sink. I think they are still good. Try them. What else?"

"We might go to the library … or the park. Maybe we will go down to the beach. It's so sunny I don't want to stay inside."

"We could walk to the beach." Twanna thought that was a good idea. "Mr. Finch would enjoy that, wouldn't you boy."

She patted his head. He gave her a dog grin.

"Fine! Maybe you would like to take some sandwiches with you. It's a pretty good walk to the beach." Roland seemed very helpful this morning. "Just be careful while you are in this neighborhood. Once you cross Clarke Street you'll be in a nicer area."

"What time should we be back?" asked Jaylin, the obedient.

"Who's going to fix supper, you or me?" asked Roland, the sly.

"I will, if you want me to," said Jaylin, a little sullenly.

"Nah, I think, since you usually do fix supper, I will treat you two to a big … thick … juicy … Pizza. Homemade. How does that sound?"

"That sounds great!" Twanna burst out. Then she felt embarrassed because she had been so loud.

Roland laughed. "Go on, get dressed and get outta here."

The girls headed for the bedroom and an exciting day.

"Are we really going to the beach?" asked Twanna, the gullible.

"No, silly, we're going to get the batteries for the flashlight and go to the basement." Jaylin's voice came from inside the bag of clothes. "Here." She threw a pair of jeans to Twanna. "Look! New jeans for you!" Then she pulled out a soft, pink sweatshirt and tossed that over to Twanna also. "You've got some nice stuff here. I love that jacket."

"So do I. But you can have it if you really want it." Twanna wanted Jaylin to have the jacket, to kinda say thank-you, and to show her how much she liked her.

"Are you crazy? I can't take the jacket. Anyway, Roland always gets a new jacket for me and how would I explain it to him? He'd skin me alive. Thanks anyway, I know what you mean."

"Let's get going, okay?" Twanna was beginning to get excited about exploring the room under the ground.

"We need a special name, you know, like a code name for the room. That way we could talk about it and no one would know what we were saying.

"How about Jennifer?" giggled Jaylin.

"You nut! I mean like ... oh ... I don't know. Alaska ... or something like that."

"Sure," Twanna said, "And the first time we talk about going down to Alaska, Roland would have a cow, and ground you until you were sixteen."

"Well, what can we say that won't give it away?"

"How about calling it the beach. We live close enough to the beach, no one would be surprised if we said we were going to the beach. And we always stay a long time, so no one would expect us back soon, and I don't think anyone would go to the beach to look for us, because there are always lots of people there."

"That sounds really good, Twanna. And then we haven't told a lie to Roland. It's just our beach is a little different than everyone else's beach." Jaylin was thoughtful. "Yep, I think that sounds good."

Taking her portable radio, she went into the kitchen to look for the batteries. After locating the new batteries, she made sandwiches – peanut butter and jelly – picked out some apples from the fridge, and found the bag of chocolate chip cookies that Mrs. Johnson had left for them. Shoving things into a plastic bag, she called to Roland, "We'll be back for supper."

Jaylin fixed the flashlight. She worked on it in the closet. Roland would wonder why they needed a flashlight at the beach, on a bright, sunny, autumn day. Twanna helped by making sandwiches and packed the lunch into a plastic bag – a

71

heavy plastic. Taking it into the bedroom for Jaylin to inspect allowed Jaylin to slip the flashlight into the bag without attracting attention.

They said, "So long!" to Roland and the three of them, Twanna, Jaylin, and Mr. Finch, headed down the stairs, out the door and around the corner. They stopped at the alley and looked around. No one was paying any attention to them.

They ducked into the alley and down the basement stairs.

Stopping to listen, they were greeted with silence.

"So far, so good," whispered Jaylin.

"Yeah," breathed Twanna.

Mr. Finch just put his nose to the basement floor and found a trail of something to follow.

"Come on, let's go." Jaylin headed toward the door to the coal room. Twanna called to Mr. Finch, who was hot on the trail, zig-zagging around the basement.

He responded with a happy leap in her direction – ears and tongue flapping.

The coal room was a dirty as they remembered.

"Leave the door open," said Twanna.

"But someone might notice," responded Jaylin, trying to tip the door shut and still hold the flashlight. "Help me."

"I don't think anyone will be down here," said Twanna, but she helped pull shut the slanted door at the top of the stairs. The old wood actually let a lot of light through, but if they hadn't had a flashlight, they wouldn't have been able to see beyond the steps.

Into the dark room and over to the other door, they cleared away the coal they had piled up and opened the other door. Down the stairs and into the underground room, they scurried.

As Jaylin flashed the light around the room, the girls

realized it wasn't as large as they had first thought. But it was loaded with boxes. There was one other object covered with a sheet, which turned out to be a chair that matched the couch. With the stronger light they could see that the couch and chair were both worn. They didn't care. They liked having someplace to sit.

"These are really comfortable. I could sleep here." Twanna had the couch.

"I like this. It's like having our own house."

"Well, should we try boxes?"

Jaylin, in charge of light, was pushing some of the boxes around and exclaimed,"Oh! Look!"

Twanna carefully made her way over to where Jaylin was and could see something very dark that reflected the light from the flashlight.

It was a huge old China cabinet. The glass in the doors shot the light back at the girls. Next to it, under a dozen boxes, was a huge old dining room table, with legs that had feet!

Both girls laughed as they saw the feet, and Mr. Finch barked. The sound almost deafened them. It was so loud in such a small area. It even surprised Mr. Finch, who jumped and looked around.

"I wonder if there are any chairs with the table," Twanna thought aloud.

"Let's open the boxes."

"Good idea!"

Both girls were really in to this by this time. They had forgotten the outside world. All that was real for them was this wonderful treasure filled "cave." Jaylin braced the flashlight on a shelf of the China cabinet, facing it toward the boxes. It was feeble in the tiny room. But, of course, better than nothing.

The first box was filled with blankets and quilts. Some old

clothes were packed in the bottom and the girls had fun looking at the tiny waists and the long pantaloons.

"Look at the lace. It sure is pretty." Twanna liked frilly things.

"Look at this!" exclaimed Jaylin. She had pulled a green satin dress out of the box. It had been very beautiful, with lots of black lace and feathers. The hat that followed was obviously meant to go with the dress. It was not crushed because it had been in a hat box. The feathers were not as feathery as they once were, but it was still elegant.

The next box they tackled was packed with tissue wrapped glass. They found plates, cups, saucers, fancy stemmed goblets and beautiful sparkling cut glass bowls. The faint light seemed to catch the cut glass items and dance around the entire piece. The dark of the rest of the room only made the glass pieces sparkle more.

"The light is getting dim," Jaylin noticed.

"Huh?" Twanna was half into a box.

"The flashlight. It's going to go out. I have two more batteries in the lunch bag. Where's the lunch?"

Jaylin was concerned about being in the dark with all the "beautiful old glass." One stumble and treasure would shatter. She knew some of the pieces had to be valuable. They sparkled like diamonds – maybe they would be worth as much.

"Over on the couch. Oh, don't move the light! I can't see!"cried Twanna. She had extracted herself and a long, tissue wrapped object from the box.

Jaylin turned back toward Twanna, flashing the light into Twanna's eyes.

"Ouch, that hurts!" Twanna turned her head away. She pulled the paper away from the object. She screamed as she turned from the light toward what she was holding.

Two eyes sparkled back at her.

Jaylin screamed!

"What's wrong?" she called. She had screamed because Twanna had.

"Oh, I almost dropped it!"

"What?"

"This doll!"

"OH! She's beautiful!" gasped Jaylin.

The doll looked at them with lavender blue glass eyes, that had a depth that made her look alive. Her blond hair hung in ringlets and she was dressed in white with a burgundy sash.

"Awesome!" Neither girl had ever seen any doll as beautiful as the one they now held.

They were breathless. They were both silent, staring at the doll. Both lost in their own thoughts about her, and themselves.

"Put her on the couch," Jaylin directed. "Be careful. I think she's glass."

"No, she's porcelain. Sometimes they are called bisque dolls. I read a book about a doll like this one. Her eyes are glass. That's why they look so real. Doesn't she look real? I mean, she really looks real!" Twanna couldn't stop talking about how real the doll looked, as she very carefully settled her on the couch.

The flashlight flickered, the light turned a little more yellow.

"I've got to change this now." Jaylin found the lunch bag and pulled out the batteries.

"Wait!" said Twanna. "We're going to be in the dark as soon as you start to change the batteries."

"I know," said Jaylin.

"Well, don't drop the new ones or we'll never find them."

"Yeah, you're right. I've got to be really careful. Come here and help, okay? You hold the new ones while I open the flashlight."

75

"I'll hold them just the way they're suppose to go in. You know, the bump end first."

"Okay, let's do it."

They were as silent as it was dark. The only noises that could be heard was the sounds they made dumping out the old cells and plopping in the new ones.

Even Mr. Finch was quiet.

The flashlight worked. It was brighter than ever and both girls gave sighs of relief. Mr. Finch curled up in front of the couch and tucked his nose under a paw.

"Let's eat lunch now," suggested Jaylin. "I just want to look at the doll."

"What do you think her name was?"

"Is," corrected Jaylin.

"Well, we'll have to give her a name but I don't think we'll get the same one."

"How about Abigail? That's an old time name."

"No, it needs to be French, or something foreign."

"Emily? Bridget? Monica? Monique?"

"No. No. Shh, and let's think." Twanna needed to concentrate.

The girls were quiet. The room was quiet. Mr. Finch began to snore. Both girls laughed and he woke up.

"Let's eat." Jaylin handed a sandwich to Twanna. Twanna peeled off her crust and gave it to Mr. Finch, who begged by flopping down on the floor.

They ate quickly, both realizing their time in the light was limited. As they put wrappers back into the bag, Jaylin said,"Let's unpack another box."

"I don't know. I'd kinda like to save some for another day."

"Oh, we will! Look how many boxes there are! It took a long time to unwrap the dishes."

"Okay. Let's finish the one that had the doll."

"You do that one. I'll start this one."

Once again Jaylin placed the flashlight on the China cabinet shelf. Twanna, instead of crawling into the box she had been working on, tipped it on it's side. Something thudded as it tumbled toward the opening.

Out came a small trunk.

"Look at this! A doll trunk!" she cried.

Sure enough, as soon as they opened it out spilled doll clothes. It was a small steamer trunk. It had coat hangers and drawers. They set it on its end, opened it up and began to pull open the small drawers.

They found treasure.

One drawer was filled with old jewelry. Beautiful necklaces, rings, and pins, made of all sorts of stones – some looked like diamonds, others like rubies and emeralds. There were blue stones that the girls didn't know the name of and even a couple of things with yellow stones.

The next drawer was filled with doll dishes, wrapped in tissue paper. Some were chipped and they didn't all match. They had been played with, washed and finally put away for good, packed carefully for someone to unwrap and play with in the future.

What would the person who so carefully wrapped the dishes think if she knew that they were in the hands of two girls, in a room no more than a hole underground? This person would most likely be the same person that played with the doll. The girls were thoughtful and lost in imagining who she had been.

The next drawer was very thin and held only doll shoes and old stockings. They were shoes for the doll. The last drawer was very deep and held more doll clothes. It held underwear, slips, some pinafores and a couple of hats. It had two fancy hats and a doll quilt. All the stuff had been played with, nothing was brand new. Some of the clothes had even been mended with tiny stitches sewed by hand.

Looking through the jewelry, Jaylin found a locket with a letter engraved on it. She couldn't tell what it was. There was also a little bracelet with a name on it. It said JUMEAU.

"I've found her name!" Jaylin was really excited. She almost jumped up and dumped the stuff in her lap on the floor. She grabbed it just in time.

"Oh, don't dump that drawer! We'd never get all those jewels back!" Twanna said.

"Opps," Jaylin said, still scrambling to keep stuff from flying all over.

"So – we know her name. I'm going to try it out." Twanna shoved stuff back into the trunk and felt her way into the darkness toward the doll. It was strange, but Twanna felt she knew her way around without the light.

"Hello, Jumeau," she addressed the doll.

The doll said nothing.

"I don't think she likes it. I think she would rather be called Rose."

"Twanna, how do you know?"

"She said so." Twanna was half joking and half serious.

Jaylin looked in Twanna's direction. *Is she serious?* she thought. Aloud she said, "She needs a fancier name than that. Something like … oh, I don't know … Julliette, or something."

"Well, lets get a dictionary and look at names. We don't have to decide now," Twanna said. "I'll call you Rose," she whispered to the doll.

"What did you say?" Jaylin was already unpacking another box.

"Nothin'. How many boxes are left?" She wanted to just

hold off and enjoy the doll and her things.

"Lots," came the muffled reply. "WOW! Look at this!" Jaylin emerged from a box with a small metal box in her hands. "It's heavy."

"Let's guess before we open it," suggested Twanna.

"Money!" said Jaylin.

"Jewels!" said Twanna.

They opened the box – Buttons! Every size, shape and color. Some very old, some only old, but all of them buttons. Some looked like pearls with stems.

"Do you know what these are?" asked Jaylin.

"No, I don't think so."

"They are collar buttons. Men used to wear shirts without collars and they put collars on and ... eh ... buttoned them somehow. I'm not sure how but that's what this is."

They put the button box aside. Next they pulled out an old crock with a picture of a bird on the side. Inside the crock were some more kitchen stuff. Knives, forks, spoons, all black and green.

"Yeck! This is dirty," said Jaylin.

"Nope. It's tarnished!" Twanna was glad she could identify the black mess. "And, I think we are looking at sterling silver!" She pretended she was eating, with her little finger crooked and her nose in the air.

"You think so?" laughed Jaylin. "How will we ever get it to look good?"

"There's silver polish in the store. It takes a lot of rubbing to make it shine. I've seen it in the movies and on TV."

The flashlight flickered.

"That flashlight is better than a clock! We're going to have to get back because that's all the light there is for now."

"It can't be very late! We just got here," Twanna moaned.

"Well, the flashlight is our guide, we must follow its instructions. It is the Master of our universe, we must follow its…"

"Oh, be quiet! I get the drift!" Twanna laughed.

"Should we put all the stuff back?" asked Jaylin.

"We don't have time and why should we? No one's going to be here."

"Maybe we should take something to the pawn shop. Mr. Wright will tell us if it's worth anything."

"I don't like him," said Twanna. "But Mr. Gordon would tell us." She brightened. Mr. Gordon was the jeweler and a very kind old man. He always said 'good day' to her and really looked at her, not through her the way most adults did. She liked to look at the jewelry behind the bars in his shop windows.

"Okay, but we'd better take something small. He might wonder if we stole it."

"No, I don't think he would. But he would wonder where we got it. We'll have to think up a story of some kind." Twanna was thoughtful.

"Well, we could kinda tell the truth. We found it."

"Okay, but where? We sure don't want anyone around here."

Both girls were quiet as they looked through the drawer of jewelry. Twanna picked out a gold ring with two blue stones and a white one.

Jaylin picked out a pair of earrings but put them back. Instead she took a necklace that had rhinestones with one large red stone in the center of the design.

"That's really big," Twanna said, doubtfully. "How would someone just 'loose' that?"

"Okay, lets take your ring in and if it's nothing special we'll take in the necklace. Do you think he may be willing to buy it?"

"I don't know. But you know that old Mrs. Bigelow has that antique shop. She might give us something for it."

"Okay, let's go while we can still see."

The flashlight was flickering more now.

Neither girl wanted to leave. They both felt at home in this hidden room, under the ground.

CHAPTER NINE

Saturday evening at Jaylin's was fun. Roland had fixed a homemade pizza with everything on it. Twanna spent more time picking toppings off then she did eating. But the crust was great! After supper they played games. Roland had an old Clue game which they enjoyed. He liked to play games and work jigsaw puzzles.

"I've got a surprise for you two," he said when the Clue game was finished. He went to the closet and brought out a big box. It had the picture of a castle on it.

"Wow!" Jaylin knew what it was right away.

Twanna had no idea but said, "Wow" also.

Roland placed it in the middle of the kitchen table.

"Come on," he said, "Let's get busy!"

Twanna looked at the picture on the box. Then read what it said. A 3-D jigsaw puzzle. You can build a castle.

"Oh, I've seen pictures of these! They really look nice. Is that what we're going to do tonight?" she asked.

"Well, I don't think we will finish it tonight," Roland

laughed. "But we're going to start it."

The 3-D puzzle kept them busy for a long time although it seemed like just a few minutes. Roland glanced at his watch and said,"Oh, I guess it's late! It's way past your bedtime. Scoot!"

"But…" Jaylin started.

"We just started," Twanna complained.

"No ifs, ands, or buts! Get going. Off to bed!"

Reluctantly they headed for the bedroom. They were actually very tired. It had been a busy day. Before they fell asleep, they whispered plans for the next day.

"Should we skip Sunday School?" Jaylin wanted to know.

"No. Mrs. Peters will be looking for us. She's the little kids Sunday School teacher."

"What about church?"

"I like to sing." Twanna wanted to be in the choir. She loved to sing.

"Me too, but I'm not as good as you."

"And I'm going to go to Mrs. Peters for supper. Are you coming with me?"

"I don't know. Let's see what happens. Maybe Roland will let me. I'll ask. Tomorrow. Good night. Today was fun."

"It sure was," Twanna yawned.

Silence descended. Sounds of a city night could be heard muffled by the protection of the apartment windows. Trains, cars, sirens, buses stopping to pick up or let people off. The autumn moon rose, yellow and huge in the night sky. But two sleepy girls did not see it. They were dreaming about the treasure in "their" room deep under the building in which they slept.

Mr. Finch was the first one awake on Sunday morning. He ran into the bedroom and grabbed the blankets from the bed and pulled them into the front room. The girls woke up because they quickly became cold. The beautiful autumn weather had changed during the night. The wind was cold and the apartment windows did not offer as much protection from the wind as they had from the sounds of the city"Oh, I don't want to get up! Where's my blanket?" cried Jaylin, rubbing one eye.

"Mr. Finch! Bring those back!" cried Twanna.

But Mr. Finch just grinned, his tongue out of the mouth grin, and looked at them from the doorway.

"I've got to take him out," Twanna mumbled. She slid out of bed and went to the bathroom. She washed her face and looked around the small room. She liked Jaylin's cozy bathroom. It was painted bright yellow and even though there wasn't a window, it looked sunny. Fish swam across the wall and the shower curtain.

"Hurry up!" came a desperate call from outside the bathroom door.

"Oh, I'm almost finished," Twanna replied with her mouth full of toothpaste.

Back in the bedroom, she dressed quickly, grabbed her new jacket and called to Mr. Finch. Without waiting for Jaylin, Twanna ran down the stairs and out of the building. She and Mr. Finch raced around the building to the back alley. Mr. Finch found a lot of good smells. He finally took care of business and they both headed back to Jaylin's apartment.

Jaylin had the table set and the smell of fried eggs and bacon filled the air.

"Hi. How about a cup of cocoa?"

"Oh. Jaylin, it's cold out there."

Roland turned around from the stove. He put a plate of bacon and a plate of fried eggs on the table. "Take off your jacket, Twanna and wash you hands," he sounded grumpy.

Twanna hurried to obey.

She and Jaylin exchanged glances.

"What's eating him?" Twanna's glance asked.

Jaylin didn't know.

Breakfast was quiet. Roland put down his cup of coffee and looked at Twanna.

"Oh Oh," she thought.

"Twanna, I heard something last night from Mrs. Johnson. I'm not sure you know yet, but I think you should. And ... well, ... I guess I'm going to tell you," he hesitated.

Roland had their undivided attention, as he took another drink of coffee and put his cup carefully down.

"Your stepfather has left. I don't know what that means to you but you'll be going home tonight and I thought you'd better know. If there's anything I can do ... er ... just tell me ... okay? I'm sorry, Twanna, I know your home life isn't the great American dream ... but I don't know anybody's whose is. I just thought you should know." He came to a halt.

Twanna was dumbfounded. She just sat there and looked at him. She didn't seem to be able to grasp why he was so concerned. She hardly ever even saw her stepfather. With him gone there wouldn't be any fighting. Her mother would probably be drunk all the time ... Who would pay the rent? Would they have to move? A very tiny voice said to Twanna, "Now you can stay away all the time."

A plan began to take shape in her mind.

"You Okay?" asked Roland.

"Yeah, uh, thanks for telling me, I guess."

Roland nodded his head but his eyes were watching

Twanna's expressions. He thought, "She's up to something. I hope it works."

Sunday School was always fun. The singing and seeing other friends. Then the bells would peel out and Twanna would be transfixed until the carillon music was over. She saw Mrs. Peters as everyone was leaving church and waved to her. She wanted to ask if Jaylin could come with her but was afraid to. If Jaylin just showed up with her, Mrs. Peters wouldn't be able to say no.

"What are you going to do?" Jaylin asked as they walked back to Jaylin's apartment. Mr. Finch had waited for them, on the front steps of the building.

"Go to Mrs. Peters for supper. What about you?" Twanna didn't know what else to say. She hadn't decided if she would tell Jaylin about her plan. If Jaylin didn't know then she wouldn't be able to tell anyone if she was asked where Twanna was. *She'd guess,* Twanna thought, *I know I would.*

"No, you know what I mean."

"I'm going to run away from home. Jaylin, no one will know I'm gone."

"That's what I figured you'd do. I've been thinking. You know that room…"

"That's what I was thinking!" interrupted Twanna. "Boy, we sure think alike."

"I can help. I can bring you food and clothes, flashlight batteries and…"

"Wait!" Twanna tried to stop Jaylin. "I'll need a lot more light than just a flashlight. I'll need two or three and I'll take my Mrs. Peters clothes, so I'll be okay that way. But I'll need very little food. I can eat at school."

"School? What do you mean school? If you run away you

won't be going to school," Jaylin stated.

"Will so." Twanna stuck out her chin. "I'm only running away from home, not from school, not from my life. I can't miss school. Then someone would know I was missing."

"Well, maybe that'll work." Jaylin was doubtful.

"We've got lots of plans to make."

"Well, lets start now."

They had arrived at Jaylin's and were going into her apartment.

Roland was on the couch watching TV.

"Hi, young ladies, what are you up to today?"

"Nothin'," Jaylin said.

"Right!" Roland laughed.

"Can I go with Twanna to Mrs. Peter's for diner today?"

"Who's Mrs. Peters?" Roland sounded doubtful.

"She's the cook at school. She lives next to the church."

"Oh, I've seen her. I heard she had about 30 some children. She could in that house. And probably still loose some."

"She has how many kids?" Twanna asked.

"Oh, not all her own. She's some kind of foster parent. I don't think she is now." Roland went back to watching TV.

"Can I go?" Jaylin persisted.

"Sure. I'll find some left-overs to fix. Some of my friends will be here anyway. It would probably be better if you weren't here," Roland said thoughtfully, looking away from the TV. to Jaylin. "Be home before dark."

The girls went into the bedroom to plan – and get Twanna's clothes. They put everything back into the big plastic bag.

"Let's take this down there now," Jaylin suggested.

"No. We'll leave for Mrs. Peter's early and leave it then."

"Okay. I'm goin' to look for more batteries."

They scrounged around until they had assembled three

batteries. The cells didn't look as if they were very good.

"I'll need new ones. Do you have any money? I could pay you back later."

Jaylin began scrounging again, this time for money.

"I've found $2.97 so far. Now, I'm going to try the couch."

Roland laughed as Jaylin pushed him from one side of the couch to the other.

He thought she was very enterprising to locate money in the cushions. She found another $1.14, all in change.

It was almost time to go to Mrs. Peter's for dinner. They planned on stopping at the corner store to get batteries after leaving Mrs. Peter's. They were going to leave the bag of clothes in the coal room door. No one would think it was anything but garbage.

They came out of the basement and turned toward the street. There stood three boys. Twanna ducked under the porch steps and pulled Jaylin in with her.

"It's Martin," she whispered. "Don't let him see us," she prayed silently. Jaylin was quiet. Mr. Finch came dashing out of the basement area and stopped dead to look around. Twanna and Jaylin tried to hand signal him to be quiet. He wagged his tail. They tried to hand signal him to go away. He wagged his tail. They tried to hand signal him to come to them and hide. He barked.

Twanna and Jaylin peeked between the risers of the stairs and saw Martin and his pals look around. Martin saw Mr. Finch.

"Hey, there's that dog that peed on me. I'm gonna teach him a lesson. Wanna watch?" Martin started toward Mr. Finch.

"Leave him alone, Martin. You're gonna do somethin' stupid and then Al will know and we'll all be in shit." One of the boys put out a hand to stop Martin.

89

Martin shook him off and reached into his coat pocket. He pulled out a gun.

"Shit, Martin, are you NUTS? What the hell you gonna do, man. You want all the cops to be here?" The other boy started walking away down the alley. "I'm like, not here, man. Not for some stupid dog." He turned and disappeared into a backyard.

"Come on, Martin, don't be stupid, man. If the cops pick you up on this, you're gone, man. We've got a big sale goin' down. Don't blow it, man."

Martin stopped. He pointed the gun at Mr. Finch. "Bang!" he said. "You're right man, some f'n' dog ain't worth it." He turned quickly, and they both disappeared into another backyard.

"Whew!" Twanna and Jaylin hugged each other. "I thought … Twanna, I thought…"

"Me too," was all Twanna could say.

"He's got a gun, Twanna. What should we do?"

"I don't know. But I'm afraid of him, even without a gun. He can be so mean…" She stopped because she didn't want to think about him anymore.

"He saw Mr. Finch here by the basement. Do you think he'll come back to look for him? Do you think he'll remember later?" Jaylin was really worried.

"I don't know. But if he's gonna get high maybe he'll forget?" she said, hopefully.

They approached Mrs. Peter's house slowly, looking at the wrought iron fence, the huge flagstone porch and steps, the towering three stories with leaded glass windows winking at them with colors of the rainbow. The front door was massive. There was a window in the door. They looked through into a small room and at another door. The second door had glass that shot colors back at them. Leaded glass seemed to be in every window of the whole house.

"Wow!" They looked at each other. This was a mansion! They both loved to read books about houses like this one. Now to be able to go inside one, wow.

On the front door was a brass lady's hand holding a ball. Twanna picked up the hand and let it fall. It hit a brass plate and a loud clank sounded. She did it again.

"That's a knocker," she said. "It's really neat, but I wonder if it can be heard inside?"

"Maybe there's a door bell."

"I don't see one." They both looked around the door frame but didn't see anything that looked like it might be a doorbell.

"Oh, my goodness! Have you been here long?" Mrs. Peters came through the inner door and wiping her hands on her apron opened the outside door for the girls.

"And you have Beau with you. I didn't know where he could have gotten to these last few days." She pointed to Mr. Finch.

"Oh, is he your dog?"

Twanna was surprised.

"Well, not really. I've been feeding him because he looked so lost and hungry. And my Butler seemed to like him. I thought he'd found a home."

"He adopted Twanna," Jaylin said. "He doesn't go very far away from her."

"Is it okay if he stays here on the porch?" Twanna was sure he wouldn't leave anyway.

"Oh, he can come in if you want him to," Mrs. Peters was standing off to one side, to let the girls in.

"I think he will stay there." Twanna looked at Mr. Finch, who was lying down, looking up at her. "Is his name Beau?"

"I haven't any idea. It's just what I called him. Come on in, come on in."

They stepped into another world. A world of wood, hand carved banisters, stained glass windows, Oriental rugs, and fire places.

"This is the foyer," said Mrs. Peters. "I love this old house. My parents had it and my grandparents before them. I've tried to keep it up – but it's a lot of work for one person."

The foyer was wood – from floor to ceiling. Huge wooden panels covered the walls. On one side was a staircase that turned its way to the upper floors. There was a fireplace, a huge window and doors to two other rooms.

Mrs. Peters pushed one French door into the wall. It disappeared. Twanna and Jaylin looked at each other.

"This is the front parlor. It's for receiving guests and since you are guests come on in." Mrs. Peters smiled at them.

The front parlor was not huge, but it had a fireplace also. It wasn't paneled with wood, but was a warm pinkish color and had roses all around the ceiling. The furniture looked old and Jaylin nudged Twanna.

"Look at the couch." Twanna knew what Jaylin meant. It looked like the one in the underground room. In fact, a lot of the stuff in the parlor looked like the treasures they had found.

Mrs. Peters was standing by another set of doors. The girls watched as she pushed one of them into the wall. Beyond the doors was another room, with a fireplace, and more comfortable looking furniture. There was a TV in this room.

"This is the back parlor," Mrs. Peters said. "Where we actually live. The front parlor really is just for company. Come on through here to the kitchen."

They followed her through the back parlor into a very large kitchen. Cabinets seemed to stretch from floor to ceiling. There was a huge stove in the center of one wall and the smells coming from it were mouth watering. There was an enclosed back porch and looking through the window on the door was the biggest dog they had ever seen.

"That's Butler. He's a Great Dane and friendly as a kitten. But don't tell anyone. Everyone around here is scared silly of him, and these days I like that. Come on into the dining room."

They went through a small room that had lost of cabinets and through a swinging door into a dining room. Another fireplace, a large table with about eight chairs, and two cabinets filled with curios.

There were three places set on the table. There were plates, glasses on tall stems, shinny silverware and candlesticks with lighted candles.

"I thought you'd bring Jaylin." Mrs. Peters smiled. She liked the looks on the girls' faces. "Well, how would you like to help carry the food in? When I was a girl, we had a butler to serve us. Now if I asked my Butler to bring in food it wouldn't get very far." She laughed at her own joke. "I like having a Butler." She continued to chuckle.

They all traipsed back into the kitchen and helped Mrs. Peters get the mashed potatoes, fried chicken and corn into various bowls. They also had Jell-O and fruit salad. Mrs. Peters poured red punch into the long stemmed glasses "to look like wine."

They sat down to a meal served in a fantasy setting. The chandler covered in glass baubles handing down, and sparkling, reflected light. The candles flickered and made the darkening windows mirrors of a wonderland that the girls had only read about.

Dinner started out quietly, everyone seemed lost in their own thoughts.

"You've always lived here?" asked Twanna.

"Yes. I wasn't born here in this house, but my mother was.

I was born in a hospital, and so were my children, but I've lived here since I was about five days old. Oh, I've been other places, but I've always lived here. I don't keep all the rooms up anymore. I even spend nights down here in the back parlor sometimes. But when my children come home at Christmas and other times, I always have room for them."

"How many children do you have?" asked Jaylin, helping herself to another pile of potatoes.

"Oh, I've had 23 children."

"What? How did you do that?" Twanna stopped with her fork mid-way to her mouth. She looked at the dining room table. No way could 23 people fit.

"Oh, not all at once! I've been a foster mother for 20 different children, at different times and for different lengths of time. I believe the most we had at one time was, oh, let me see," she began counting on her fingers, as she mumbled names to herself. "Yes, there were fourteen at one time. Three of mine and eleven others. But that only lasted two weeks. Then three little ones were placed for adoption and the two oldest reached eighteen and struck out on their own. We had nine for a few months and then in one day we had two newborns and one teenager. That was Johnny. Poor Johnny. He was beyond our help, I guess. He kept stealing and finally ended up in prison. He's the only one that didn't seem to be able to control himself. It's a shame. He was smart, too. Well, you can't succeed with everyone. But it bothers me sometimes. Maybe if things had been different for him … but that's another story. I could just go on and on about my children. They all have good jobs and most have families. My own three live a long way away. I miss the kids. I miss the noise and the laughter. That's why I work at the school. I can see and hear children. That makes me feel good."

Jaylin and Twanna both understood. She worked there

'cause she wanted to not because she had to and that's what made her different. She loved the kids and they could tell.

When supper was finished and they were all so full they could hardly move, the girls started to clear the table.

"I can do that, you don't need to help," Mrs. Peters protested.

"But we want to," exclaimed Twanna.

"No, I have nothing better to do this evening, you do enough around the kitchen, I'm sure. Let's go into the front parlor and visit."

"Well, as long as you have a Butler to help put things away," Jaylin joked.

Sitting in the front parlor was like sitting in a different century.

"Did all the kids keep this room nice?" asked Twanna.

"Oh, we had lots of other places for them to play. We just used this room at Christmas. We used to move all the furniture back against the walls and have a tree so bit it touched the ceiling. One year, we couldn't even use the room because the tree was so fat we couldn't get around it without knocking off ornaments. We would have another tree in the upstairs playroom. That one had all homemade ornaments. The kids would start weeks in advance and make ornaments. It was as much fun getting ready for Christmas as Christmas morning itself. I wish those times were back."

"Do you have any grandchildren?" asked Jaylin.

"Oh, my, yes," she laughed. "I hear from so many of my foster kids and their kids. My own grandchildren are almost grown up. There are eight of them. The others, well, I'd have to get out my book and look up the number. I think it's somewhere around sixty. The babies, you know, the babies that only stayed a couple of months when they were real little, well, I don't think they know who I am, even. I don't hear from them. But I gave them the love they needed when they needed it most. A little baby needs love to grow. I think it's as important as food to them, I do."

They talked until they heard the bells from the church next door, begin to ring. On Sundays there was a concert of the bells at 8:00 p.m. As soon as they heard the bells, Jaylin said they had to leave. Mrs. Peters did not keep them. She got their jackets and gave each one some leftovers for "a snack." She also gave Twanna a container of food for Mr. Finch.

As they left, they stopped at the front gate and looked back. Mrs. Peters was at the door watching.

"That was even better than I thought it would be," Twanna said.

"She's really nice. I don't know too many old people who can talk like she does. I mean, she says things that are interesting. And what a house! Some of those things are like the stuff in the room!" Jaylin said.

Twanna was thoughtful. "I wish I had a home like that."

"Well, tonight you will have your very own room. And take my food, too. If you get hungry you'll have a snack. Don't use the flashlight too long or you won't have any light in the morning. I'll come and get you – I'll get up early so you won't oversleep. Do you think you'll be scared?"

"I'll have Mr. Finch with me. That'll make it okay." Twanna tried to sound brave, but was a little scared. "What will you say if someone comes to your home looking for me?" she asked Jaylin.

"I'll tell them I saw you leave at about 8:30 to go home. That's not a lie. I just hope they don't ask if I know where you are. That'll be harder to fool them. Anyway, do you really think someone with look for you?"

"Not tonight. My mother will be drunk and my brother won't notice. With my stepfather gone, no one will know if I'm there or not." She wasn't sure she liked the idea of not being missed, but it made it easier to hide in the underground room.

They had reached Jaylin's apartment building and went around to the alley. They went into the coal room, found the bag of clothes right where they had left it, pulled out the flashlight, then faced each other.

"Thanks, Jaylin."

"Be careful, Twanna."

"Good night. See you in the morning."

Being in the underground with Jaylin had been scary. Being there alone was terrifying. She knew no one was there except Mr. Finch and herself. She would be able to hear someone else breathing. The silence was profound. No city noises filtered into the blackness. She flashed the light around. She knew she had to work quickly.

"Rose, you can sit on this chair," she said aloud. She jumped at the sound of her own voice. It was so loud! But it was nice to talk to something.

"We have to find blankets, Mr. Finch, and then we'll go to bed. Oh, I almost forgot." She quickly got the container of food for him and put it on the ground. He made nice noises as he gobbled the food down. She turned the flashlight away from him and he still ate, so she knew he could find food in the dark.

Glancing over the boxes, she moved to the one that had linen and stuff in it. She pulled out two blankets and a sheet. She spread the sheet on the couch and spread out the blankets. She looked for a pillow and found a small one she could use. She quickly undressed and put on a pair of Jaylin's pajamas.

"Thanks again, Jaylin. Goodnight Mr. Finch. Sleep tight."

She crawled onto the couch, straightened out the covers and turned out the flashlight. She put it under her pillow toward the inside of the couch. She had just curled up in a cozy ball when she felt a thud at the opposite end of the couch.

"Oh, Mr. Finch! You scared me!" She laughed. "I guess you like blankets too." She had turned the flashlight on to watch Mr. Finch nose his way under the covers and thump down with only his nose showing.

"Goodnight, again," she whispered.

All was very quiet. Steady breathing from opposite ends of the couch filled the darkness, broken only by whimpers now and then as animal and child dreamed their own dreams.

CHAPTER TEN

Twanna's eyes popped open.

"Where am I?" she thought, panicked because it was pitch black. She was too frightened to move. Something had touched her cheek. Something wet and soft and...

"Oh, Mr. Finch!" Twanna realized he had licked her face to wake her up. Relief and memory flooded her mind. She reached under her pillow for the flashlight and turned it on.

"There's no clock! I don't even have a watch. We forgot – how can I tell what time it is?" she wailed.

Getting up and dressing as quickly as she could, her mind active as to the problems she would encounter. School, food. Had anyone looked for her? Had Jaylin been questioned. No one was here so Jaylin had not told anyone where she was. Safe so far.

She wore clothes that she would wear for school. She also put on a jacket. Mr. Finch bounced and jumped ahead of her to the doorway. Twanna turned off the flashlight and tried to make it through the coal room door. She only bumped into one wall.

And she could see light at the other doorway, the one to the basement, so it must be morning.

"Twanna!" came Jaylin's voice in a loud whisper.

"I'm ready," Twanna called back.

They met at the door.

"Well, how was it?"

"Well, did anyone ask about me?"

"Nope!"

"It was okay. Mr. Finch sleeps under the covers!"

"Let's go to school. We'll be in time for breakfast." Jaylin turned to leave.

"We need another flashlight. I'd like two."

"We can see if we can buy one. I have to wash clothes today after school. You could bring yours and help me."

"Okay. I was wondering what I could do about that. And I've got to go to the bathroom."

"Oh, I forgot! There's one down here! It used to be the janitors closet. It's got a sink and toilet and some really old mops. Come on, I'll show you."

Sure enough, at the opposite end of the basement was a small closet with a toilet and a deep old sink.

"Yuck! It's dirty!"

"We can scrub it tonight. Can you wait until we get to school?"

"I'll have to!" Twanna crossed her eyes.

They laughed.

School presented no problems. Twanna's day went as usual until about 2:15 when a messenger from the office appeared outside the classroom door. Mrs. Edwards stepped outside to speak to him.

"The office wants to see you, Twanna," she said as she

stepped back into the classroom.

Twanna looked at Jaylin. Jaylin shrugged her shoulders. Twanna rolled her eyes, got out of her seat and headed toward the door. She turned toward the stairs that would take her down to the first floor where the office was located.

The office consisted of the principal's office, the assistant principal's office, the Social Worker's office and the Nurse's office. There was a large central area where two secretaries worked behind a long counter.

Twanna could see into the main office through the window on the door.

There sat Martin.

Twanna went to the other end of the hallway, to the drinking fountain. She wanted to run! How could she go into that office with Martin there? She couldn't.

Twanna went back to class. She sat in her seat and didn't say anything to anyone. Mrs. Edwards didn't ask, just nodded at her as she entered the room.

A messenger appeared at the classroom door. Mrs. Edwards stepped outside the door for a discussion with the messenger.

"Twanna, come here please."

Twanna slowly, very slowly got out of her seat and strolled to the door.

"Where did you go a few minutes ago?" Mrs. Edwards wasn't really cross, just puzzled. "To the office," mumbled Twanna.

"The office said they haven't seen you."

"Yes, em."

"Did they see you?"

"No, em."

"Where did you go?"

"To the office."

"Okay, Twanna. What's going on?" Mrs. Edwards put her hands on her hips and looked at Twanna.

Twanna knew she would have to tell her something.

"I forgot to go in?" she tried.

"Twanna!"

"I looked through the window and saw my cousin, Martin." Twanna hung her head.

"Well, what's so awful about that?" Mrs. Edwards was very much in the dark.

"I can't go near him," Twanna mumbled.

"What did you say? Talk up please."

"I'm scared of him. He hurts me." Twanna was looking at the floor, speaking so softly that Mrs. Edwards wasn't sure of what was said, but suddenly she began to understand. As the horror dawned on her, she gasped.

Twanna looked up at her with a defiant look. "I won't go with him. I won't go near him. No one can make me!" She turned to run but Mrs. Edwards had already reached out to hug her – the hug turned into a grab – the grab turned back into a hug. "Twanna, no one is going to make you go anywhere with him! Come with me, I'm going to take you to Mrs. Bailey. She will help more than anyone else."

Mrs. Edwards, with Twanna's hand in hers, stopped at the next classroom door to ask Mrs. Fairview to watch her class while she was gone. Mrs. Fairview looked at Twanna with a surprised expression and said, "Sure, no problem."

Mrs. Edwards continued to hold Twanna's hand all the way down the stairs and into the office.

"Come on, Twanna. We gotta go. Your Mama's looking for you." Martin stood up from the bench and moved toward them as she and Mrs. Edwards entered the main office.

"Get back!" Mrs. Edwards stepped between Martin and

Twanna, pulling Twanna behind her. "Don't you touch her!" she ordered.

Twanna wasn't sure but thought she heard Mrs. Edwards say "sleeze bag" under her breath. She was so surprised she forgot to be scared.

"We want to see Mrs. Bailey, right now!" Mrs. Edwards had turned into a protector.

The secretary, already out of her seat, said, "Okay. I'll get her." She wondered what had happened to turn nice Mrs. Edwards into such an aggressive person. She actually thought Witch, but that wouldn't really apply. These thoughts passed quickly through her mind as she went to the Social Worker's office.

"Mrs. Bailey? A mess for you!" she said very sweetly.

"What's up?" Mrs. Bailey appeared at her office door and moved quickly into the main office. Her thin bird like appearance and manner emphasized her anxiousness.

"This young man is ... has, well, has caused Twanna some grief. I think perhaps you could talk to Twanna?"

Twanna was almost pushed through the main office into Mrs. Bailey's room. While this was happening, Mrs. Riley, the principal appeared. She also moved into Mrs. Bailey's office.

Martin ran out the door and they could hear him running through the hallway and out of the building.

All the adults looked at each other.

"We wouldn't have released her to him anyway," Mrs. Riley said. "What made you think we would?" She looked at Mrs. Edwards and at Twanna. They looked at each other and Twanna smiled a shy smile of thanks to Mrs. Edwards. Mrs. Edwards squeezed her hand.

"I was shocked, I guess. I'm very upset about what Twanna has told me and I over-reacted."

"No, it's understandable." Mrs. Bailey patted Mrs. Edwards on the shoulder. "Don't worry. I'll handle it now."

Mrs. Edwards tried to let go of Twanna's hand – Twanna hung on and sent her a pleading look.

"It's okay, Twanna," Mrs. Edwards said as she used her other hand to release Twanna's grip. "Mrs. Bailey will help. You are not in trouble."

"I think I'll just leave this to you. My presence isn't helping." Mrs. Riley looked at the other two adults. Nods were exchanged and she went back to her office.

Twanna found herself in a big wingback chair of blue velvet. It felt like velvet, anyway and it was so big if she pressed herself back into the back she knew she was hidden from view. She liked the chair.

"…if you want to." Mrs. Bailey had been talking to her.

"Huh?" She felt so stupid for not paying attention.

"Do you want to talk to me?"

"Not really."

"We need to talk about Martin, at least."

"He hurts me." She wasn't going to say how – she wasn't!

"Can you tell me more?" Mrs. Bailey's voice was soft and kind. "I just want to help you, Twanna, that's all."

"No."

"Are you sure?"

"Yes."

"Are you going to be okay?"

"Yes."

"Do you have a way to get home?"

"I walk with Jaylin."

"Will Martin bother you?"

"I don't know. But I can run real fast!"

"I'm sure you can." Mrs. Bailey smiled. "If he shows up –

run to the police station."

"Why?" Twanna had never thought of that.

"Because what he is doing, or what I think he is doing to you is illegal and he can be put in jail. If you talk to me about it I can help you. Do you want to talk?"

Twanna was tempted. Mrs. Bailey was so kind maybe ... The bell rang.

Twanna shot out of the chair before she realized what had happened.

"I've gotta go," she said.

"Twanna, don't shut me out. I can and will help you. Do you understand?" Mrs. Bailey was coming toward her as she was heading toward the door.

"Okay. Maybe. I've got to get my coat and books. Please!"

"Go, Twanna." But Mrs. Bailey felt she should have kept her. *If anything happens it's my fault,* she thought as she watched the young girl scurry through the office and into the hall.

"What happened?" Jaylin was jumping up and down, she was so curious.

"Oh, nothin'." Twanna had appeared outside the building and watched Mr. Finch and Jaylin jump. "You're acting like Mr. Finch!" Twanna laughed.

"Don't change the subject! Why the office? What happened? What did you do?" Jaylin was persistent.

"Well, Martin came to school to get me."

"Oh, Twanna! No!"

"I saw him and didn't go to the office. So they sent for me again. Mrs. Edwards took me to the office herself. Mrs. Riley said they wouldn't let Martin take me home. And Mrs. Bailey wanted me to talk to her. I didn't. She said what Martin did to me was illegal. Is that true?"

"What does he do to you?" asked Jaylin.

Twanna realized she had said too much.

"Scares me."

"I don't think scaring you is punishable by law," said Jaylin. "Mrs. Bailey is wrong." Jaylin dismissed the thought and Twanna said nothing more.

Back at school Mrs. Bailey was busy writing up a report, with notations to follow up with a home visit. Mrs. Edwards was at her desk, worrying.

Mrs. Riley was writing on her appointment calendar – Conference with Mrs. Edwards re: Twanna Michells.

CHAPTER ELEVEN

The trip to the Laundromat was boring. Washing clothes was usually fun, but as Twanna and Jaylin entered the laundromat, loaded with two baskets of dirty clothes, they saw Walter's mother and knew that they were doomed. Walter's mother talked a lot – and always about herself. She was a make-up salesperson and all she talked about was how she felt, how she looked, how she reacted to something in her life … and to fifth grade girls it was boring. Actually, it was boring to everyone. They spent the wash cycle listening to how she "adjusted to all the changes that were happening" in her life. They spent the first drying cycle listening to "how horrible" Walter's attitude was, but "it's just like his father's attitude." By the second drying cycle they had quit listening and were just watching the clothes tumble in the dryer. Finally it was over. Even slightly damp jeans couldn't get them to stay another cycle. They just dumped the clothes into the baskets and took off. Walter's mother was still talking.

"Do you think she knows we left?" giggled Jaylin.

"I don't know. But she probably doesn't care."

"I had so many things to talk to you about, and I didn't dare say anything. I didn't want to take the chance of being heard."

"What did you want to say?" Twanna asked.

"Well, what about the stuff we wanted to take to sell?"

"I don't know. I'm afraid that they will think we stole it."

"Could we ask Mrs. Peters?"

"What do you think she'd think? Where would we have gotten stuff like that?"

"Well, we need to come up with a story, 'cause I'd like to know if that stuff is good or not. Wouldn't you?"

"Yeah, but, I don't think I want to sell it. I kinda like it being there, you know, like it all belongs together." Twanna was trying to explain a feeling she didn't really understand.

"But if it's worth a lot of money, then you wouldn't have to worry about how to get food and stuff."

"Okay, I know you're right. I just…"

"I know." Jaylin stopped talking to pick up some clothes that had fallen out of the basket. Mr. Finch was carrying a towel.

"Look at Mr. Finch. He's helping," laughed Twanna.

"Yeah, but who's towel does he have? It's not ours," Jaylin said. They started to really hurry, and somehow couldn't stop giggling about Mr. Finch stealing a towel.

Once again Jaylin accompanied Twanna down into the basement and to the coal room. Once again they said goodnight at the door and Twanna disappeared from sight into a world of blackness. If Mr. Finch hadn't plunged happily into the darkness, Jaylin would have been depressed.

That dog is so happy … everything has to be okay! she thought to herself as she climbed the stairs to her nice warm apartment, where she could lie in bed and read with the light on. Or she could make hot cocoa in the bright, warm kitchen.

As Twanna settled quickly for the night, in her circle of light, she was thinking how lucky she was to have a place to sleep, in peace. No noises, no yelling, no one pushing her around, no one hurting her. Just Mr. Finch, who would protect her from anything, and the beautiful glass eyed doll ... she felt very happy.

The darkness became her friend.

Jaylin knew something was wrong the minute she opened the apartment door. Something inside tightened up and she felt afraid. She didn't know what it was, but she also wanted to run. She didn't. She went into the kitchen and looked around.

Things were a mess. Dishes had been thrown around and broken pieces were all over the floor. The refrigerator door was open. The table was shoved to one side and a chair had been knocked over.

The front room was worse. The books were all off the shelf, the couch was a mess and the TV was all static.

"At least that's not broken," Jaylin sighed.

"Huh?" Roland was sprawled in the recliner with a can of beer.

"I've finished the wash. I'll hang the clothes up and then I'm going to bed. Do you want to sleep in here so I can have the bedroom tonight?" was what she said. What she wanted to say was, "What the heck happened? What's your problem?"

"Okay. I'm drunk. Go to bed. I'll talk to you tomorrow."

"At least he's not mad." Jaylin was relieved. She knew that when an adult gets really angry anything can happen. Once, long ago, she had seen Roland angry. It was right before her mother had died. Roland had yelled and thrown things around. Her mother just sat and cried. Jaylin could remember it just enough to be afraid. She knew she didn't understand what had happened, but she also knew she never wanted to see Roland angry again. She very quietly put away the clean clothes, cleaned up the broken dishes and tumbled into bed. She lay in the dark and listened to the snoring of the stranger in the living room.

"Jaylin. Jaylin. Wake up," Roland called from the door of the bedroom. "Time to get up for school."

"I'm up," Jaylin said as she snuggled down into the covers.

She just wanted another five minutes, then she could get up and ... Suddenly she was wide awake. Had she overslept? What about Twanna? Complete memory came flooding back and she looked up at Roland.

"Come on, honey. I was awful last night. I'm glad you weren't here to see it. I'm really sorry that I made such a mess. Thanks for cleaning it up. I don't have any excuse for acting like that. I'm a grown man and should be able to control my temper ... but, Jaylin, I have some really bad news and I don't know how to tell you. I guess just straight ... eh? You're such a brave little girl, and you've had so much to do ... Well, I don't know, but life just isn't fair." Roland turned toward the kitchen.

Jaylin sat up in bed and rubbing her eyes, said, "What's up?"

"I am. I mean my job is up. They are closing the plant and I've been laid off." Roland sounded funny.

"You can get another one. You've got a great record." Jaylin tried to sound normal, but her voice was strange.

Roland turned around and came back into the bedroom. He sat on the edge of the bed and gathered Jaylin into his big strong arms.

"Honey, I'm not young anymore. I will have a very hard time getting another job. There just aren't a lot of jobs for people like me, no education, no talent, just a strong body that's getting older. But I don't want you to worry. I'll do everything I can to keep us together. I promised your mother that I'd take care of you, before she left. I will send you to your aunt if I have to. You will be okay." He hugged her.

"But I don't want to go to Mississippi! I want to stay here and take care of you and TWA ... of you," she wailed.

"Oh, you little sweetie! Always taking care of people." Roland chuckled and rubbed Jaylin's head. "Come on, get up for school. We'll see what we'll see."

"What are you going to do today?"

"Go to work. I'm still there for awhile. Then I do get vacation pay and unemployment. That's what makes me angry. I don't want unemployment. I want all that money that I paid into retirement that will be gone. That's not right, that's just' not right." As he spoke, he began to get angry.

He turned and looked at Jaylin, took a deep breath, and grinned. "I'm okay," he said.

Jaylin scurried out of bed, got dressed and beat it out the door. She needed time to think about the new developments in her life. She was so preoccupied with her problems, she almost forgot to stop for Twanna. When she remembered, she had already passed the alley and was headed for school. She quickly turned around and as she started back toward the basement she saw Twanna standing there looking at her.

"What's wrong?" were Twanna's first words to Jaylin.

"Everything! Maybe I'll move in with you." Jaylin was really down in the dumps.

"That's be fun!" Twanna really meant it. The two of them could live in the underground room just fine. They would have to figure out a way to get some money, for food, and batteries.

Jaylin wasn't paying any attention to Twanna. She was walking quickly, with her head down, lost in her own thoughts.

"What happened?" Twanna tried again.

"Roland lost his job," Jaylin muttered.

"Can't he get another one?" Even as she asked the question, Twanna knew that jobs were not easy to get.

"He doesn't know. And he's really worried. And angry."

"Are you okay?" Twanna didn't know how to ask her if Roland had hurt her. She knew how she would feel if someone asked her about her family.

"No, he's really nice. It's just that, well … if he doesn't get a job then he's gonna send me to Mississippi, to my aunts. I don't want to go!"

"Well, move in with me. Mr. Finch and I would love to have house, or rather cave, guests. Really, Jaylin, you could just move in with me."

"Twanna, unless we quit school and just stayed down in that hole, Roland would find me. It'd spoil that room for you, and I won't do that."

"Maybe we can figure something out, like, if you say you're going to your aunts and you stay with me instead." Twanna was hopeful. She couldn't imagine life without Jaylin.

It began to sink into Twanna's head. Jaylin might be going away.

Who would she talk to? Who would be there for her? She would have no one at all. Mr. Finch would be the only living thing who would know where she slept, and no one would care.

They walked to school in silence, both lost in their private misery.

Walter was absent. Twanna and Jaylin were so self absorbed that they didn't notice Marvin, standing by himself in the playground looking lost.

"He's not here," Marvin announced as he approached Twanna and Jaylin.

"Who's not here?" Twanna came out of her mood long enough to ask.

"Walter. You know, Walter. Our friend? Remember, there are people other then you on this planet." Marvin sounded angry. "Well, do you know why? Maybe he's got the flue."

"No, he never gets sick. He hasn't ever been absent from school. Remember? He had perfect attendance since first grade."

"Call him after school. It must be really serious for him to stay at home." Jaylin was interested now also.

"He's not here. What can I do?" Marvin was a best friend without his partner.

Twanna and Jaylin looked at each other, then quickly looked away. They were very close to tears. This is how they were going to feel if Roland didn't find a job.

"At least you have a home! And a mother!" Twanna almost shouted at Marvin. She turned and stamped toward the school and got in line.

"What's that all about?" he asked Jaylin.

"We're not happy either," was all Jaylin would say.

Mrs. Edwards was not in the room. The class sat down and looked around. Maybe there would be a substitute teacher today. Some of the kids would like that, but Twanna and Jaylin wanted the security of having Mrs. Edwards there today.

The entire class became silent as soon as they saw Mrs. Edwards. She was crying.

A teacher crying?! That just didn't happen. They weren't suppose to cry. They weren't suppose to do anything that humans did. They were teachers.

Mrs. Edwards sat down behind her desk. Another strange move … she never sat behind her desk. She put both hands up to her face and sighed. She took her hands down and looked at the class.

"Good morning, boys and girls. I'm sorry to have to tell you that Walter is in the hospital. We don't know when he will be back to school. This afternoon we can make cards for him, which I'm sure he would like to have. Now, let's get started…"

"Mrs. Edwards, why is Walter in the hospital?" asked Marvin. "Is he really, really, sick? Does he have cancer?"

"No, Marvin, he doesn't have cancer. That's all I can tell you for now. Let's get started with reading … Angel, will you begin with Chapter two…"

And so the day began … with trouble everywhere except in the warm protective environment Mrs. Edwards created for her students.

The whisper went around the room after recess. Twanna heard it before Marvin and didn't pass it on. She thought that Angel had started more trouble. Jaylin passed her a note asking if she had heard what the kids were saying. Twanna nodded her head when Mrs. Edwards was writing on the chalkboard.

"That's not so!" Marvin stood up and shouted at Bill. "He did not! I would know! I'm his best friend! He just gave me his pocketknife! His favorite one. He'd tell me if…" and he burst out crying. He turned and ran blindly into the cloak room.

Mrs. Edwards was astounded.

"What has been going on?" she demanded.

No one answered.

Silence was present.

"Well, if anyone wants to go to recess, or even go home tonight, someone had better tell me what has been going on!"

"Marvin doesn't believe it, but Shirley said that Walter's sister told her that Walter tried to kill himself." Mary Ellen never could keep a secret.

"What?" Mrs. Edwards was speechless.

"That's what we heard." Bill looked very guilty.

"Okay," Mrs. Edwards paused and looked undecided, and worried. "I suppose I will have to tell you the facts, and then maybe Mrs. Bailey will come and talk to you."

She paused and walked over to the windows. She seemed lost in thought as she looked out over the crowded city streets and toward the lake in the distance.

"Yes, class, Walter attempted suicide. You all know he is having a really rough time at home because his father has left and he mistakenly feels it's his fault. I really don't know what to say to you all, except that he is going to be taken care of and helped so this won't happen again."

"But why didn't he tell me?" came a voice from the cloakroom.

"Marvin, he did tell you, but you didn't hear him. He gave you his favorite knife. Would he do that normally? You just didn't understand what he was trying to tell you. He was saying good-bye, don't forget me. I think I'd better send for Mrs. Bailey."

Recess was spent in the room, talking about feelings. Mrs. Bailey listened and all the students talked about how they felt about Walter and how they thought they would feel if they had been in Walter's shoes. Marvin finally came out of the cloakroom and took his seat in the classroom. Mrs. Bailey said it was okay to be angry with Walter, and it was okay to be hurt. She said it would be good to talk about how they felt. She also promised not to tell anyone what they said. And they trusted her.

After school, Mrs. Riley walked into Mrs. Bailey's office and sat down. Mrs. Edwards was already in the wingback chair and Mrs. Bailey was behind her desk.

"Not an easy day," commented Mrs. Riley.

"Nope. And would you like to hear the rest?" Mrs. Bailey was shuffling papers around.

"Can I avoid it?" asked Mrs. Riley and gave a short laugh.

"I don't think so. It's about Twanna, so Mrs. Edwards, I want you to hear this also. She has no family. She has no home. I don't know where she's staying, but no one knows where she is after school. Her mother is an alcoholic, and I mean serious. Her stepfather left and the brother is a drug user. The rent hasn't been paid and the landlord is going to have their things put on the street this weekend. But no one has seen Twanna. It seems as if she has been forgotten. I was so angry when I left that place this morning. And then to go and talk to Walter's mother about … well, about her … she couldn't even get off the subject of herself now, after this! What a day!"

"What can we do about Twanna?" Mrs. Edwards was really concerned. "She's always in school, and she looks nice, since Mrs. Peters gave her those clothes…" she wasn't sure she should have said that.

"I'll have to report my findings to the authorities. But with the way they work, it may be months before anything is done. Maybe I should talk to Jaylin's family. I know those two girls spend most of their time together. Maybe her family knows what is what."

"Her family consists of a stepfather, who is not her legal guardian. He was living with her mother when she died, and has taken the responsibility of raising her. We have known this for a long time but since she appears to be well taken care of, haven't reported it to anyone. I certainly wouldn't want to upset

116

a good situation. But, maybe, when you talk to him about Twanna, you can get a feel for what's happening for Jaylin also. We have some needy kids here, don't we?" Mrs. Riley shook her head.

"We need to do something for them," Mrs. Bailey said softly.

"But what can we do?" Mrs. Edwards said, sadly.

The walk home from school was very quiet for Jaylin and Twanna. Even Mr. Finch didn't jump as high, or pull on Twanna's coat. He walked along, every once in a while he would try to look into Twanna's eyes, as if trying to figure out what was wrong.

Twanna wanted Jaylin to ask her to come up to the apartment, but Jaylin really wanted to be alone, so she didn't say anything.

Twanna went quietly into the basement and started toward the coal room, with Mr. Finch close behind. Mr. Finch suddenly whirled around and froze. Twanna was so lost in her own thoughts she didn't notice until she heard the long, low growl that came from deep inside Mr. Finch.

"Nice doggie, nice doggie. Here, doggie, have a nice piece of meat doggie. Take a nice long nap, doggie. Twanna wants to play with Cousin Martin."

Twanna was trapped! There was no where to run! She was cornered! Straight ahead was the coal room and then the underground room, but she couldn't get there without Martin seeing where she was going. She couldn't turn around and run past him because he would grab her. She had to think of something. She had to.

Mr. Finch wasn't taking the meat that Martin was holding out to him. But he was inching closer and closer to it. He was also still growling and crouching closer to the ground. Twanna could tell that he wasn't going to take the meat. Maybe she could get around Martin and run for the outside door. Maybe…

Just as she thought that, Mr. Finch sprang. He went right for Martin's face. Martin jumped back, dropped the meat and swore at the dog. He reached out to grab the dog and Twanna shot past him, running for all she was worth. Mr. Finch was right next to her. She ran out the door, down the alley and headed straight for the police station. She could hear Martin running after her but didn't take the time to look back.

She just ran.

When she reached the police station she began to slow down. She looked behind her and couldn't see anyone following her, not even Martin. *Safe … this time,* she thought. She was going to have to be more careful about going into the basement. Martin had almost found out where she stayed. If he knew she would not be safe.

She sat down on the park bench in front of the police station. Reaching down, she petted Mr. Finch, silently thanking him. He understood, as only dogs can, and thumped his tail in reply.

Twanna was hungry and she knew that he was also. To refuse to take that meat had been hard for a hungry dog. He really was hers. And she was his. The bond of friendship was firmly sealed. But what about supper?

"Come on, Mr. Finch, let's go home." Twanna knew where to look for change and all she really needed was a candy bar. That would be enough for her, and there were still some scraps for Mr. Finch. They didn't smell very good, but he wouldn't mind.

Twanna heard the commotion before she saw what was happening. She heard the sirens of the cop cars and then saw the boys running. One ran right at her, but wasn't even seeing her.

He shot past and ducked into a yard, jumping the fence to do so. She heard a scream and then a shot, followed by another scream. The place was alive with boys running and police running after them.

Mr. Finch did not leave her side. Twanna flattened herself against a fence and waited. More shots. More sounds of running. When all seemed quiet, she resumed her walk toward the small store around the corner from Jaylin's apartment. Once around the corner she could see what the trouble was. The owner of the shop was lying in the street, and there were people all around him. There were three police cars and two officers.

One officer was talking into a walkie-talkie and the other officer had Martin.

Twanna couldn't believe her eyes. There was Martin, with handcuffs on! He was squirming around and around, but couldn't get out of the officers grasp.

"Well, we got one of the gunmen," Twanna heard one officer say. "If the old man dies, this one will too."

"I saw the whole thin'!" An old lady, in house slippers and curlers in her hair, was telling one of the police men. "I've seed this youn'en afore now. His is always trouble. His is just no good. Always sayin' foul stuff. And this time with that gun, uh, uh, his is always trouble."

"Well, ma'am, I'll need you to testify in court. Are you willing to do that?"

"I certainly is. If we'ns can get this one off'n the streets, we's all got a better chance of sleepin'." She nodded her head until the curlers threatened to fly out of her hair.

Twanna slipped quietly out of sight and walked quickly back to the apartment building. She looked around to see if anyone was hiding in the basement, but Mr. Finch seemed to think it was all clear, so she went into the coal room ... and almost died of fright.

She saw something in the darkness move. She tried not to but she screamed. The object screamed too.

"Twanna! You scared the life out of me!"

"Jaylin! What are you doing, trying to kill me?"

"I heard all the sirens and was worried about you." Jaylin sounded hurt.

"Martin. They got Martin! Jaylin, I'm safe!"

"What did he do?"

"Some lady says he shot the owner of the little store. The police have him in handcuffs."

"That means he'll be gone."

"I know! I'm safe. But, Jaylin, I don't think he did it. He was here, trying to get me. Mr. Finch jumped into his face and I ran to the police station. I thought he was chasing me. How could he have been robbing a store?"

"Maybe after? Did you see him chasing you, or did you just run?"

"I didn't look back. You know that slows you down too much. I just ran."

"Well, maybe he didn't chase you."

"But, maybe he did." She was very upset. "There was another guy in the alley that had a gun. I heard him shoot after he jumped a fence."

"Well, someone will report that. Let the police take care of it. Twanna, you don't want him around you, do you? You know he's trouble."

"But, what if he didn't do this?"

"He sells drugs, right? He attacks kids, right? Oh, you thought I didn't know? Well, he attacked Amy, that little three year old right down the block, and no one could do anything about it because Amy couldn't tell what had happened. She can't talk, but she sure does scream every time she sees him ... tell me he didn't do nothin' to her." Jaylin was indignant.

"I didn't know about that." Twanna was surprised. She had been so concerned about her own safety she hadn't though about Martin attacking anyone else. She felt stupid. And Jaylin had known about Martin all the time.

"Why didn't you tell me you knew about Martin?"

Jaylin looked at where her feet would be if she could see her feet. "I figured you'd tell me when you wanted to."

"Thanks."

"Are you okay? Oh! I brought you a couple of sandwiches."

"Oh, Jaylin, that's really fantastic. I'm hungry."

"You always are," Jaylin laughed. "I've gotta get home. Roland will wonder were I am. See you in the morning."

"Goodnight, and thanks again."

CHAPTER TWELVE

The days seemed to hurry by. Twanna spent her nights in the darkness and her days at school. The darkness became more and more comfortable, and the room proved to be warm when the fall winds blew cold. She and Mr. Finch curled up together on the couch and snuggled in the blankets. She was happy and at peace.

Saturdays were spent going through boxes with Jaylin and running in the park and on the beach with Jaylin and Mr. Finch. Sundays were spent in church and then at Mrs. Peters. She invited them to lunch many times and the stories she told kept them coming back for more. They were going to explore the attic but never seemed to get up there. Life was fun.

On a bright fall morning, when everything was crisp and clear, Jaylin showed up in the coal room with tears in her red-rimmed eyes. As soon as Twanna saw her in the daylight, she asked, "What's wrong."

"I've got to pack."

"Why? Where are you going?"

"To Mississippi. Oh, Twanna! I don't want to go!"

"No! You can't go! What will I do without you?"

"There's nothing I can do. Roland doesn't have a job and the unemployment is going to run out. He's afraid that he won't be able to get work and we will end up on the street. He says that my Auntie wants me to live with them. They have a house and lots of room. Yeah, with nine cousins? I'll bet!" Jaylin sounded very upset.

Twanna was silent. It hurt too much to talk. Jaylin was going to leave her. Jaylin was going to a place she would be able to call home.

Jaylin was going to forget her just the way everyone else had. She walked quickly with her head down.

Jaylin hurried to keep up, stumbling because of the tears.

"Twanna. Don't walk so fast," she complained.

"Just go on away! Just go on! You're going away anyway, you might as well go away now," Twanna cried and started to run ahead.

Jaylin just stopped and watched, crying silently.

The next day, Twanna refused to go to school. Jaylin begged her to come but Twanna just stayed on the couch in the dark. Jaylin didn't dare miss school. The teacher would call Roland and he would wonder where she had spent the day. So she left Twanna and Mr. Finch and walked to school alone.

"Twanna, you've got to go to school. Mrs. Edwards was so surprised that you weren't there. She had Marvin take a note to the office that said she wanted your mother called. Marvin told me at lunch. He said the office said that they waited two days before they called. So, you've got to go. They will know your mother isn't there. And then they will begin to ask where you are, and they will ask me. I'm not real good at lying. Twanna, promise you'll go with me tomorrow. Please."

"We'll see," was all Twanna would say, from beneath the blanket.

Jaylin went back to the apartment. She was really worried about Twanna.

Should she tell Roland? What if Twanna wouldn't come out at all? She couldn't just move away and leave her in that basement. What should she do?

"Down in the dumps?" Roland asked.

"Huh? Oh, yeah, I don't want to pack."

"I know, honey, I know. But it'll be for the best. You just wait. You'll have so much fun with those cousins. You'll see." Roland didn't sound too convinced himself.

Jaylin had stopped listening and was thinking about Twanna.

"…Twanna and all," Roland was saying.

"What?" Jaylin knew she had missed something.

"I just said that I knew it was going to be hard to leave Twanna, and all. Where are you, Jaylin. You look as if your mind is already in Mississippi. You know, the weather is a lot warmer there. There won't be any snow to shovel," he said. *Or to build snowmen with, or slide down hills on, or to make angels in,* he thought, walking away.

Jaylin worried through supper. She worried as she began sorting clothes. She told Roland that she wanted to leave her heavy winter clothes for Twanna. He had agreed. She worried herself into bed, and worried herself to sleep.

"Twanna, you've got to come to school today!" Jaylin was desperate. "You just get up and get dressed!"

"I'm dressed. I just don't feel well. I'm cold. I want to stay in bed. No one will care. You'll see. I'm just going to stay home today. I'll get up tomorrow."

Jaylin thought she sounded drugged. "Are you okay?" she asked.

"No. I'm sick. Leave me alone. I'll be okay tomorrow, I promise."

"Have you had anything to eat?"

"I'm not hungry, I'm sick. Leave me alone. Won't you be late for school?"

"Oh, Twanna, what am I going to do? I don't want to leave you like this. Do you have a fever?" she tried to find Twanna's head under the covers, but Twanna jerked away from her groping hand.

"I said leave me alone! I'll be okay tomorrow."

"Twanna, come on with me. I don't have many days left before I have to leave. Come on. I miss you. School isn't any fun without you there. Come on," she pleaded.

"Tomorrow. I'll come to school tomorrow." She huddled deeper into the blanket.

Jaylin turned to leave and saw Mr. Finch sitting by the outside door of the coal room. "Has Mr. Finch been outside?" she asked.

"Yeah. Good-bye."

Jaylin worried her way to school. She worried her way through all her school work and through her lunch. Mrs. Peters watched her as she took her tray to an empty table and sat by herself. She wondered where Twanna was.

Twanna kept her promise. The next morning when Jaylin ran down the stairs and into the basement, there stood Twanna, blinking oddly in the bright light of day.

Jaylin gasped.

"What's the matter?" asked Twanna.

"I'm just surprised to see you. And glad, too," she said.

"I promised I would come back to school today. Let's

pretend that you're not going away. Please. I don't want to think about it, okay?"

"Sure, if that's what you want." Jaylin was still upset by the way Twanna looked. She just didn't look right.

When Mrs. Edwards asked Twanna for a note from her mother, Twanna said she had forgotten it. She told Mrs. Edwards that she had been sick but was feeling better. Mrs. Edwards looked at her and started to say something, but didn't. *I wonder what she thinks. I wonder if she believes me.* Twanna thought, as she turned away from Mrs. Edwards eyes and went to her desk.

"Angel, take this note to the office, please." Mrs. Edwards was sealing an envelope. "And it had better be sealed when it gets there. I will be checking," she said firmly.

Angel flounced out the door.

Everything seemed normal. The class got busy on Math and the silence was one of busy children learning.

"Well, I never! Did you see that little face lookin' at them from the winder? I never seen such a sad sight, not in all my born years. I declare, how come, when they has so much trouble goin' on, they gots to put a po' chile like that in a police car." Mrs. Bertha Watts was fuming, as she tied her apron around her ample middle.

Mrs. Peters looked up from the apple dumplings she was arranging on the tray. "What's that? Something happen?" She was used to Mrs. Watts and her complaining about social conditions. She really didn't listen to her too closely.

"That lil' chile. You know'd. That lil' thing that you like so well. Whas her name? Tianna? Treena? Somethin' like that."

"Twanna. Did something happen to Twanna?" Mrs. Watts had Mrs. Peters full attention.

"Yes. They tooks her away in a PO-leece car. That lil' thing, lookin' out that winder. Makes a body want to cry. What could she have done."

Mrs. Peters didn't wait to serve lunch. She took off her apron and headed toward Mrs. Riley's office. Her face didn't look cheerful and her manner wasn't kindly. Thunder was about to be heard by someone.

The secretaries were all ears, as Mrs. Peters began to voice her opinion of the "goings on" of the Social Worker and the "authorities." She couldn't believe they had taken Twanna away in a police car. She knew that the authorities thought they were doing what was best for Twanna, and Twanna would be placed in a Foster Care home, but while she was waiting for an opening she would be held in the detention home for girls. She would be exposed to all ages of girls who had been convicted of crimes and who were runaways. Mrs. Peters knew what that place was like. She had taken several of her girls from there, and although that was a long time ago, some things just don't change.

"Time to call in favors." Mrs. Riley thought she heard Mrs. Peters mutter, as the older woman hurried to the door. "And time to make decisions."

"Bryan, you know I wouldn't ask you to interfere if it weren't something real serious. This little girl doesn't belong there in that place. You've got to do something. Shari will tell you how awful it was. She had nightmares for a couple of years and she was only there one night. Pull some strings. Do some paper work. I don't care what it takes. You know I have more money than I need. Just get that child out of there."

"But, Mother Peters. Where do you suggest I put her?" Bryan was really tired and he didn't know what to do about his former foster mothers request. Maybe she was getting senile, or something. To interfere in a proceeding like this was just not like her.

"My dear child, you can place her here with me! You know I'm still registered for Foster Care. You know I'm on the emergency list. Why haven't you used me lately? Think I'm getting old, or senile?" She seemed to still be able to read his mind, and it shook him up. Maybe she was right. Maybe she wasn't getting old. Maybe he was getting hardened.

"Bryan, you always do what's best for the children you deal with, I know that. This time I know what's best. Now, get that girl out of that place before they close for the night! Please?"

"Mom Pete, I'll look into it right away. But you know you can't keep her because of the rule about family. You must have a husband or at least there needs to be a male figure in the picture, and…"

"Bryan, you worry about getting that child to me, and I'll worry about getting a husband. Just hurry up!"

CHAPTER THIRTEEN

Twanna found herself all alone, sitting in a large room that looked like Mrs. Peters foyer. She was on a bench by the door and could see outside.

"If only I hadn't gone to school today," she thought, and her eyes filled with tears.

Voices could be heard coming through the door that had closed behind the police woman after she had instructed Twanna to "sit on that bench and don't move."

"What have I done?" Twanna asked in a small voice.

"I don't know, but if you are brought here, it must be pretty serious." The police woman rolled her eyes. "Personally, I can't imagine you doing anything wrong, not with those big innocent eyes. But I guess I'm wrong."

Twanna heard the heavy front door open and looked in that direction. A tall, young man stood inside one set of doors and a bell sounded in the office across the hall. The lady in the office checked who the person was and then pressed a buzzer. The door clicked and the young man came into the hall.

"Are you Twanna?" he asked her.

"Yes." She was afraid to not answer.

"So, you're the one causing Mom Peters to go into orbit. I'll bet you don't know the trouble you've caused," he said. He didn't sound angry, but sounded as if he was teasing.

"Yes, sir," was all Twanna could manage to say.

The young man laughed and said, "Let's get this straightened out now." After knocking sharply on the door to the other office, he entered without waiting to be invited in.

Another sound at the door. Twanna turned to watch a very pregnant girl wait to be admitted. The girl was looking intently at her. She seemed to want to say something, but couldn't. She kept nodding at the door with her head. As Twanna sat there and looked at her.

The girl finally came over and said very loudly, "I've juss got to sit down." Then in barely more than a whisper, "I've left the door open. I put gum on the latch. The outside one isn't locked. RUN. Don't stay here. Run, kid."

Twanna looked at the girl and quietly stood up. The girl nodded her head and got up from the bench. She turned to walk down the hallway and after a few steps she let out such a screech that Twanna ran to her.

"Get out of here! The clerk will help me. I'm okay, kid. It's a distraction. How dumb are you? Run."

She screeched again and the door of the office across the hall flew open, but so did the door into which the policewoman and the other man had disappeared. People came from all directions. It was chaos. Twanna backed away from the crowd, and quickly ducked out the door. She thought she heard someone shout at her but she didn't stop. She flew down the stairs, out the huge front gate and into the welcome crowd of people going home after a hard days work, not caring that a little girl was running for her freedom.

"Where can I go?" Twanna had finally stopped running. She had no idea where she was, just that no one was behind her. She knew she was close to the lake and close to down town, but exactly where she was she didn't know.

"If I follow the beach, I know I can find my way back to the room. I can't go there tonight. I wonder if Jaylin will tell?"Deep inside she knew Jaylin would never tell about the underground room. She knew that she would be safe there. Getting there was another matter. It was late, getting cold and she could tell by the factories that she was in a rough part of town. There were people shuffling down the alleys and there were cardboard boxes all over the place. It was like a movie she had seen on TV. about homeless people. She turned and walked the other way. She tried to look as if she was heading home from a friends house. She thought if she convinced herself of that then people looking at her would think the same thing.

Head down, collar pulled up around her chin, she walked away from the lake, away from the only way she knew how to get home.

Suddenly she heard a sound which made her stop in her tracks. Bells! She could hear bells! She looked up toward the sky, but the only thing she could see were the tall buildings. No bell tower, no steeple, no welcoming carved doors of a church could be seen.

"But there must be a church. I can hear the bells. Maybe I can follow the sound."

But the wind whirled around the corners and between the buildings carrying the sounds away and bringing them back. Dancing and twinkling sounds of bells, coming and going, but never saying from whence they came. Enticing, teasing, tempting sounds of comfort and beauty, of life and freedom.

After chasing the sounds through several streets, Twanna gave up. She could still hear them, but she knew they would offer her little comfort and would not provide a place to stay for the night.

"Lookin' for the mission?" a cracked old voice sounded practically in her ear.

She jumped.

"Ha, ha, ha," cackled the old person. Twanna couldn't tell if it was a man or woman. The face had so many lines it looked as if it had cracked and cracked again. "I didn't mean to scare you, but it was fun."

Twanna turned to walk away. The old person followed her.

"If you need a place to stay tonight, the mission is just over there." An old hand with a torn glove on it pointed.

There was the church! Right there in front of her was the church and the sounds of the bells were still hanging on the air.

"Thanks," she said, "but I'm going home."

"You look lost to me." A watery eye came close to Twanna's face, and she backed away. The cackle could be heard again. Twanna turned and tried to walk as if she knew where she was going, knowing the old person was watching. She wanted to run but forced herself to walk.

The old person watched as Twanna disappeared in the shadow of the steeple.

It was getting dark, and Twanna was frightened of every sound and every movement she came across. A cat ran out in front of her and she actually screamed. Then she had to run because she was sure someone had heard her.

Where can I sleep? she kept thinking. *Where can I just lie down?*

And on she went, deeper into the city, farther from the lake and her path home.

Finally, the streets were so dark and the night so quiet that no one was around. The apartments were lighted and the warm glow from the windows made Twanna feel funny inside. It was as if she was empty and she realized that was loneliness.

"I might as well get used to it." She didn't even have Mr. Finch anymore. Where was he, she wondered. Where was Jaylin? She thought she could never go back to school and that made her very sad. Even if she managed to get back to the underground room, she would never be able to talk to anyone she knew. She would have to stay hidden until they forgot all about her. She would have to steal food from the garbage cans and maybe if she took cans in to recycle she could get some money. Maybe she would have to sell some of the stuff she had in the room.

She couldn't take another step. She stumbled into a doorway that was dark and curled up into a ball. Sleep was a welcome friend, and it came to call almost immediately.

Tumbling backwards and being stepped on is not a nice way of waking up in the morning, but that is what happened. A young woman had opened the door where Twanna was curled up and had actually stepped on her before she realized what she was doing.

"Oh, I'm so sorry! I didn't see you. Are you okay?"

Twanna was totally disorientated. Where was she? Who was this woman? Where was Mr. Finch? She looked wildly around.

"Are you okay?" The young woman was very concerned. This child looked like something from a movie, something raised by wolves or dogs or something.

"I'm fine," Twanna muttered and stumbled away from the door, away from the apartment and away from the concerned look on the young woman's face.

"Can I help you? Please? Don't run away. Let me help you."

But, of course, Twanna ran.

Twanna was aware of hunger. She was so hungry she could hardly walk. And she couldn't think of anything else. She needed to get some food. How, was the question.

Maybe I could ask someone for a dime, she thought. *No, that would be begging. I can't do that.*

"Little girl, are you okay?" a kind voice asked. Twanna had stopped in front of a bakery and was looking at the donuts in the window.

"I'm hungry." She could not lie.

"Well, do you have any money? You could buy something."

"I ... I ... I lost my money." She began to think quickly. "I'm on my way to school and I lost my lunch money. I can't go home because my mother will be mad at me." Suddenly she seemed able to lie quite easily.

"Can the sob story. I've seen runaways before. Here, have a donut and take this turnover too, it's from yesterday and I can't sell it. Just don't hang around here, okay? It doesn't look good for the shop." His voice was still kind, but some of the words were harsh. He watched as Twanna gobbled down the donut, then looked at him.

"May I have a glass of water, please," she asked with a very dry mouth.

The man laughed and got her a carton of milk from behind the counter. "Here, this is better for you. Sober up, kid, and go home, nothing can be as bad as the streets. You're way too young to be out turning tricks. You're just a baby."

Twanna thanked the man and said she was trying to get

home but was lost. He said, "Sure. I've heard that too."

"Where's the lake?" she asked.

"In that direction," he said and pointed. Then he looked at her with a puzzled expression.

"Maybe you are lost. Do you need a ride home? I could call the police…" He was talking to thin air, Twanna had fled in the direction of the lake.

She walked all day, stopping only when she couldn't take another step. Finally she saw the lake. The blue looked so beautiful she cried. The sand looked so white and soft … and it was soft. She fell down onto the sand and fell asleep immediately. When she finally woke up it was dark. She scrambled to her feet, dug the turnover out of her pocket and ate it slowly. She had no idea where, what or when she would eat again. But she had the energy of the young and turned south at the waters edge and trudged on in the darkness.

I can see really well, she thought. *I guess living in the darkness has some advantages to it after all.*

Finally she sat down to rest and realized she wasn't able to tell where she was. It was too dark to see the buildings and look for the landmarks that were familiar to her. So she decided to sleep. Sleep decided to stay away. As she lay on the beach, the sound of the water, the coldness of the air, the sounds of the city were a lullaby to her ears. Sounds, smells, soothing beyond all description. Then, a huge harvest moon, glowing bright red, then changing to orange and finally the bright white light that turned night into day, rose slowly and majestically over the lake and lit the way for Twanna. She got up and began to walk again, knowing where she was and where she was going. She was almost home.

As she walked past the school, she looked at the old building and wished she could go back there. But she couldn't, not ever.

Something moved. Something was coming at her. Something was running at her.

She turned to run, then heard a sound that caused her heart to leap. A strangled cry, a whimper, almost a bark, as Mr. Finch flung himself at her, and knocked her down.

He jumped on her prone body, grabbed at her sleeves, licked her face, jumped away from her and then back at her, licking, nipping, and rolling on her. He knew she would come back. He knew. And he would welcome her as only befitting his reason for existence.

"OH! Watch out! Yeck, you're licking me on the mouth! Ouch! You're hurting me! Your nails scratch! Ouch! Stop! Sit!"Mr. Finch sat down, but quivered with excitement.

"I'm really glad to see you, too! You've been waiting here almost two days! Oh, I love you, Mr. Finch, I just love you." She gathered the quivering little dog into her arms and they just sat that way for awhile.

"Come on, Mr. Finch, let's go home." It sure sounded good, even if it was a hole in the ground. It would be warm and safe and she would have a friend to talk to.

The sky was lighter as they reached the basement, but the basement was dark and the flashlight was hard to find. "Jaylin must have been down here looking for me," Twanna thought as her fingers closed around the flashlight handle. She didn't know if she should be glad or worried about that. She decided to not think about it right then. She found her way into the room, took off her jacket, took off the rest of her clothes, put on Jaylin's pajamas and plopped onto the couch. She discovered Mr. Finch was there before her, waiting for her to snuggle up against his warm soft body. They fell asleep together, warm and happy.

"Twanna! Twanna! Wake up! Where have you been? Everyone is looking for you! Wake up!" Jaylin was shaking Twanna.

"I'm tired. I want to take a five." She turned and burrowed down into the blankets.

"Twanna, wait 'til you hear!"

"Jaylin!" Suddenly Twanna was wide awake and sitting up. "You didn't tell about this room, did you? People don't know where I am, do they?" The terror of the last couple of days returned full force.

"No, I didn't tell anyone. I wouldn't do that. I promised," she said. "But, listen. Things are different! Everything has changed since you ran away. The Ghost came to your aid. Mrs. Peters, I mean. Mom Peters ... that's what we're going to call her from now on. See. It's okay."

"Jaylin, what are you talking about? How can everything be all right. I ran away from the police. They must be looking for me. And you are moving in just a couple of days. I can't ever go back to school ... and you say everything is okay. Are you nuts?"

"No, I mean, I said everything is different. I know I'm not suppose to tell you, at least I don't think anyone wants you to know, but I don't think they will ever find you, so I'm gonna tell so that everything can be okay." She sounded very pleased with herself.

"Jaylin, what are you talking about?"

"Okay, listen. Mrs. Peters, you remember, told us she was a foster mother. Remember? Well, she wants you to come and live with her and since one of her Foster kids is in charge of the placement department, or whatever it's called, it's been fixed. And..."

"Wait! You mean I'm going to live with Mrs. Peters? Our Mrs. Peters? In that great old house? Me? What about Mr. Finch? Oh, I bet she lets me keep him! She likes him! Me? In that old house? With Mrs. Peters and Butler, and Mr. Finch? Really? Are you sure?" Twanna was so excited, yet she could hardly believe her ears. Could this really be true?

Suddenly she remembered. "But you'll be gone!"

"No! That's one of the best things! She hired Roland as a handyman! And as part of his wages, we're going to live there too! Twanna, we will be sisters!"

They looked at each other in the dimming light of the flashlight. Could this really be true? They put their arms around each other and vowed to be the best sisters ever.

CHAPTER FOURTEEN

Twanna skipped down the long hall and into the second floor bathroom.

"Hi," she said.

"Hi," came the muffled response from under the sink. "Hand me that wrench, please."

Twanna picked up the wrench and handed it to Roland. "What are you doing?" she asked.

"Looking for the treasure map," he responded. "I heard tell it was stuck in one of these pipes, and I only have three thousand more to search."

Twanna giggled. "Well, dinner is almost ready and you'd better not be late. It's Thanksgiving!" She skipped out of the room and back down the long hall. Putting her hand on the old oak banister, walked leisurely down the stairs, imagining what it would have been like with full gowns and ... Mr. Finch interrupted her thoughts as he flew past her, with Butler hot in pursuit. And when Butler ran past he usually knocked you or anything around you down.

"Hey!" Jaylin was in the foyer and shouted at the two dogs. "Don't run in the house." And then she laughed.

"Come and get it!" Mrs. Peters was using their intercom – her voice. "Turkey's on the table." Both dogs flew into the dining room. They needed no extra invitation.

"Not you two. Mr. Finch, get off the table! You get leftovers, not first choice. Butler ... to the porch, go on, take Mr. Finch with you. Go on." Mrs. Peters could be heard pushing the unwilling monsters to the area of confinement for the duration of the dinner.

"This smells like heaven." Roland came down the stairs behind Twanna. She was surprised to see he was dressed in a shirt and tie. He had just been under the sink...

"I had coveralls over this," he said as he winked at her.

"Let me escort you beautiful young ladies into the dining room." He held out both arms. They took his arms and then tried to fit through the door, and although it was double pocket doors, it still wasn't wide enough for the three of them. They laughed as they stepped through and then were stunned into silence. None of them had ever seen such a magnificent sight. The table was set in Mrs. Peters very best china, with her crystal, long stem goblets gleaming in the candle light. The silverware shone with the brightness that only comes when sterling is newly polished. The platters were piled with food, and the serving dishes were overflowing with mashed potatoes, yams, corn, and several kinds of salads. Mrs. Peters stood in the swinging door and smiled.

"Every bit of work was worth it to see the looks on your faces," she said, and beamed.

They sat down at the table to eat and were all very quiet. Mrs. Peters said, as she bowed her head, "I think each one of us has a special thanks to give today. Maybe we should all take a turn."

As each one took a turn giving thanks for the gifts they had received, Twanna was trying to figure out what to say. Finally it was her turn. "Thank you, God, for love that doesn't hurt, for people to trust, and for all the good stuff you've let me have. Thanks for my new parents, Mrs. Peters and Roland, and for my special friend, my sister, Jaylin. And thank-you for letting Mrs. Peters, Mom Pete, be such a great cooker!"

As she finished, the bells in the old bell tower of the church next door, began their Thanksgiving Day concert. The sound was pure, and glorious in the crisp, cold air, muffled by the leaded glass windows, softened by the warmth of the food and the noise of the meal. It sounded like nothing Twanna had ever heard before. It was a new thrill, a new promise of beauty and an assurance of freedom to her young soul.

Twanna looked away from the windows and at Jaylin. Jaylin was looking at her. They smiled and winked at each other. They shared something that no one else knew. The underground room was still their secret.

The End

Printed in the United States
19231LVS00001B/421-444

9 781413 706420